BEWITCHED BREAK INN

Mystic Inn Mysteries

STEPHANIE DAMORE

Chapter 1

"You almost done?" asked Emily, one of the inn's weekend employees.

"Not even close." I worked quickly, scooping a spoonful of birdseed into the center of the palm-sized piece of lavender tulle. I pinched the gauzy fabric together and secured the satchel with a bit of thin satin ribbon before placing the wedding favor in the box with the other dozen I'd made. Thirteen were complete. I only had two hundred eighty-seven left to tackle. I groaned, thinking about the ever-expanding guest list. When ghosts decide to tie the knot, watch out. The dead knew a lot of people. I supposed it made sense. You were bound to make a friend or two when you kicked it around Earth for a couple hundred years. Percy, the inn's resident poltergeist, had recently popped the question to his girlfriend, Eleanor. The sweet older woman had been bound to our local tavern for over two hundred years. She had lived in Silverlake before our town was even incorporated. Once the curse was broken and she was set free, Percy wasted no time courting her. Who knew the mischievous poltergeist had a soft side? It turned out all the ghost needed was a good woman to set him straight. That's not to say he wouldn't occasionally leave a frog in my shoe or swap out the salt with the sugar for my morning coffee. Percy might be a reformed poltergeist, but he still was a poltergeist.

"Sorry I can't stay to help," Emily frowned. I gave her credit. The look was genuine. Emily wasn't like her high-school peers who stared at their cell phones all day. Emily worked. She was dependable, responsible, and had a positive attitude—a rare combination indeed, which was why I planned on offering her more hours after graduation. "When do you need them done?" she asked.

"A little over a week. The to-do list is never-ending," and it wasn't only because I loved making lists.

"I could cancel my plans." Emily reached for her phone in her back pocket. "It's just a quick bicentennial meeting at Carter's." Emily's voice trailed off as she began to tap on her screen.

"Don't you dare," I reached forward to stop her. "Vance should be here soon. We'll get it done." Vance had spent a long weekend at a law conference in Seattle. I'd spoken to him after his flight landed in Atlanta over an hour ago. I was looking forward to our reunion, and not just because he promised to help until the birdseed satchels were done.

"Are you sure?" Emily looked skeptical at the twenty-pound bag of birdseed and rolls of ribbon.

"Positive. And you can't miss that meeting, aren't you chairing it?" The town's bicentennial celebration wasn't for three months yet, but plans were well underway, including at the high school.

"Wait until you hear my plans for the carnival. I hope the council approves them." Emily beamed, reminding me of myself when I was her age.

"Then you're definitely not staying here."

Right on cue, Emily's ride pulled into the inn's parking lot. "Have a good time. I'll see you Sunday," I added before Emily could repeat her offer to help.

"Okay, but call me if you need anything before then," she went on to say anyway.

"Go. Have a good time." I waved goodbye to Emily while saying hello to a passing couple returning from their afternoon out. Soon the lobby was empty again. I sighed, looking at the pile of supplies. It was going to be a long night.

Two hours later, my eyes flicked over at the clock. It was just after nine o'clock, and I was nowhere near being done. I loved planning big events. Truly, I did. It was what I had done in

Chicago for years. When Eleanor asked me to plan their wedding, I immediately said yes, especially when she explained how traditional she wanted everything to be. I could do traditional. However, I forgot just how time-consuming event planning could be. Add in my daily workload, and the inn being full of guests? Well, it was a lot. Not that I would say anything to Aunt Thelma when she called. She was still spending time in Mount Holly with her boyfriend of six months, Mayor Kringle. She had recently bought a lovely cottage in the magical Christmas village after I assured her I had everything more than under control here. It had been mostly quiet in the six months since the New Year's Eve fiasco. There was nothing to report except a small break-in at the high school a few nights before, which sounded more like a teen dare than a criminal mastermind. I had to admit that I liked things quieter. It was one of the benefits of living in our enchanted town.

All these thoughts filtered through my mind as I continued to tie the wedding favors. It wasn't until after it took me three tries to tie the next satchel and bird seed spilled across the counter and rained onto the carpet that I realized I might be due for a break.

I tightened my fingers into fists and shook my hands, hoping the movement would relax my cramped joints. I then rolled my shoulders back to ease the tension between my shoulder blades and turned my head from side to side. When I was done, I glanced at my phone, which sat face up on the registration desk. Still no word on Vance, but that shouldn't be too surprising. Traffic in Atlanta could be a nightmare.

I was still thinking of reconnecting with my beau when I heard a noise coming from the back hallway. Noises weren't uncommon at Mystic Inn. Not when I had an almost full house. But something about this sound was different. It was like when a guest forgot their key card, and they pulled hard on the door only to have the deadbolt keep it in place. It was a jarring sound of metal rattling the glass door.

I leaned across the registration desk and craned my neck to peer down the hall. Someone or something darted away outside.

Without even thinking, I grabbed my wand and held it down stealthily at my side as I made my way down the narrow hallway, making sure to keep to the side in case a wayward curse found its way shooting down the hall. If the last year in Silverlake had taught me anything, it was that you should always prepare for the unexpected.

I reached the end of the hall but kept back from the glass doors for a moment, waiting at the ready for whoever the mystery guest was to reappear. After a couple of seconds of silence, I stepped closer, leaned my shoulder against the glass door, and looked out, turning my head from side to side. The fluorescent light above the door shone down on the cement pathway that led to the parking lot. This entrance was for guests assigned to rooms at the far end of the inn. It was easier for them to lug their bags from the parking lot on this side versus coming through the lobby. A neat row of arborvitaes marched along the landscape border. They were the perfect size for someone to hide behind.

A rustling noise to my right caught my attention. "Who's there?" I threw my wand in that direction and was ready to blast the intruder if need be. The bush began to shake in earnest, and I held back, waiting to see who or what would emerge when out launched a little black cat. I looked closer at the feline with a bad case of the zoomies. It darted all over the side garden, disappearing in and out of the bushes, circling the rest. Its coat blended in with the night as it turned and bolted off into the darkness.

"Wait! Come back here!" I took off jogging in the direction the cat had run off to, but the furball had no plans of slowing down.

"Here, kitty, kitty!" I tried again. I had jogged halfway across the parking lot before I even realized it. The cat leapt down the Enchanted Trail and looked like it still had no intention of stopping. I stopped giving chase and didn't even try a spell, realizing it would be useless. The cat was long gone.

He or she appeared to be on a mission. I could only hope it knew where it was going,

I sucked in a breath and tried to think if I knew who the cat belonged to. Then I shook my head. There was a slight chance that it wasn't a cat at all but a person. I knew better than anyone how things weren't always what they appeared to be. I turned into a cat myself. It was an inherited gift from my mother's side, and the trick had saved me a time or two in the past. My hand clasped the tiger's eye pendent around my neck. The pendent held the magic for the transformation spell. I never took it off.

"Who are you chasing?" Vance's voice asked from behind me, causing me to jump.

"Gah!" A silver sparkle shot out of the tip of my wand in response. Glitter rained down like confetti, sprinkling down in the parking lot. Never sneak up on a witch with a wand. Especially one that recently unlocked her powers. You might wind up cursed if you're not careful. "You scared me half to death."

Vance jumped back, knowing I was likely to swat him on the shoulder for giving me a heart attack."It's good to see you too," he replied with his mischievous smirk. "Can I kiss you yet, or are you still going to smack me?"

"I dare you to step closer and find out." The words sounded harsh, but not when I said them with a laugh. I had my hand on my chest, willing my heart to slow down.

"I'll give you a minute," Vance grinned, but then his voice grew serious. "Who were you chasing?" His eyes scanned the darkness. "Are you okay?"

"I'm not sure. I heard a noise outside, and when I checked it out, a black cat jumped out. I lost it at the trailhead."

"Was it really a cat?"

"I wondered the same thing." It was probably nothing, but you never knew around here. Stranger things have happened.

Chapter 2

The scream ripped through the evening air. Vance and I were still standing in the parking lot.

"What was that?" I turned to ask Vance, but he was already bolting down Enchanted Trail. I turned and followed him, holding my wand up as I ran.

We didn't have to go too far. Deputy Amber Reynolds was about fifty feet down the trail. She scrambled to get up and run towards us as if a bogeyman was hot on her heels.

"Are you okay?" I asked at the same time Vance asked what was wrong. I usually avoided Amber at all costs. The sheriff's daughter was rude, and spoiled, and a dozen other adjectives, but she was also a person who right now needed help. And maybe, just maybe, she'd remember I'd been there for her when she needed me the next time we faced off at a crime scene.

"There's a…there's a…" Amber stammered, pointing over to the bushes with a shaky finger.

I followed the direction she pointed in. Vance used his cell phone as a flashlight, illuminating the path. My eyes rested on a pair of white shoes sticking out from the brush.

I gulped. The reality of the image quickly sunk in. "Oh no. Vance, I think there's a dead body."

Amber nodded. "That's what it is. At least I think so," she said with a rush of breath.

Vance walked forward with his wand out, ready to defend us if need be. I kept mine out as well.

Amber got her head together. "Sorry. He surprised me, that's all."

I took in Amber's appearance for the first time. She wore a racerback tank-top, running shorts, and sneakers. Her blonde hair was pulled up high in a ponytail.

"You were out for a run?" I surmised.

"It was too hot earlier, wish I wouldn't have waited now." Amber walked back down the trail and bent low, picking up something small and white out of the wood chips. It was hard to make out what it was in the darkness. Amber blew on it and then took the matching piece out of her other ear. "I was listening to music. I didn't even see him until I tripped." Amber pocketed the ear buds and then walked over to Vance, who had bent low and examined the body.

I kept my distance. "Who is it?" I was afraid to ask.

Vance stood up. "I have no idea. I've never seen him before."

"Me either." Amber frowned. "Let me call my dad."

Curiosity got the best of me. I craned my neck and rolled up on my tiptoes. I couldn't see the man's face, but I could see his white boat shoes, khaki shorts, and blue dress shirt. If I had to guess his age, I'd say he was somewhere in his fifties. But I could be way off, given I was only seeing him from the waist down in the dim light from Vance's flashlight app, and I wasn't planning on getting any closer.

Sheriff Reynolds arrived on the scene in record time. Dr. Humphrey was right behind him. The werewolf shifter was one of our town's family practitioners and our resident medical examiner. It was different being on this side of things. Normally I was the one finding the dead bodies, and Amber and her dad would show up and question me. After the sheriff realized Vance and I had simply came to his daughter's aid when she screamed, we were free to go.

"That's different," Vance remarked once we emerged from the trail.

"I know. Not that I want to find another dead body, but it's nice not being a suspect."

Vance tugged my hand. "Are you okay?"

I knew what he meant. Stumbling upon death always was unsettling. "I am. Although I can't help but wonder who he is and how he died."

"I couldn't tell," meaning Vance couldn't tell the cause of death by sight.

"Think it might be natural causes?" I hated how hopeful I sounded.

"I'd say that's a safe bet. Come on, let's get inside."

Chapter 3

It took Vance and me until after midnight to finish tying up all the birdseed for the wedding. The repetitive task soothed my mind. By the time I fell into bed, I was dead tired. Normally, with it being my morning off, I would've slept in, but I had to take advantage of every free moment I had to work on the wedding, including getting up early before working in the afternoon. I stretched in bed, arching my back, my arms above my head. It was only after I managed to curve my torso back to an impressive degree that I realized something was up. I looked down at my fluffy, white-furred tummy and outstretched claws. Ever since I freed my magic, it seemed to be firing when I least expected it, including when I slept. This wasn't the first time I'd woken up as a cat. It was initially a bit disconcerting, even if the stretching sure did feel nice. I settled back into the warmth of my comforter, kneading the blanket just so, basking in the morning sun. My eyes slowly fluttered closed and soft purrs hummed from somewhere deep inside.

Moments like this were pure bliss, even if I'd never admit it to another living soul. But I couldn't lounge around as a lazy kitty all morning. Reluctantly, I said the spell to transform back to my normal self. Promising myself I could nap around as a cat another day.

Back in human form, I quickly got ready and headed out to Diane's bakery, La Luna. Happily, my motivation to get things done promptly came back when I was no longer covered in fur. I was supposed to meet Eleanor and Percy at the bakery at nine o'clock, but I was hoping to get there early, grab two cups of coffee, and waste a little bit of time with Misty at the bookstore. It was our morning routine whenever both of us were free and in town. Misty had recently returned from being on tour with her rockstar boyfriend Daniel, and we had a lot to catch up on.

Eleanor and Percy were originally not going to have a cake, seeing ghosts can't eat, but then Eleanor confessed she'd always envisioned having a three-tiered wedding cake, and the rest was history. They were just lucky that Diane didn't balk at the rushed request.

It turned out that I didn't have to go to the

bookstore to catch up with Misty after all. My best friend was talking to Diane when I walked in the door. My footsteps faltered when I took in her somber expression. Had they heard about the mystery man's death?

"I'm not sure what to make of it," she said to Diane as I joined them. Diane stood on the other side of the bakery counter, leaning forward.

"I was hoping the high school was a one-off type thing," Diane replied.

"We don't know if they're related, but I wouldn't be surprised." Misty then turned to me. "Someone broke into the bookstore last night."

"No! Are you okay? Is the store okay?"

Misty nodded. "That's the thing. Other than the lock, nothing else is broken."

"They didn't take anything?" I asked.

"Not that I can tell. I dropped the bank deposit off after closing last night, and the till wasn't touched."

"What about the wards?" Misty had switched to using magical locks a while back.

"That's my fault. I'd gotten lazy after being on the road, and I didn't set them. Vicki locked the front door, and I headed to the bank. Just like we did the night before." Vicki was Misty's store manager.

"I'm not going to forget mine now," Diane said, looking over at her front door.

"I'm not going to either, trust me. I called the sheriff's department, but they weren't much help. They're supposed to send someone to take a statement, but without anything stolen, there's not much they can do other than record it."

"They might be a little busy," I added. Diane and Misty cocked their heads at me. "You mean to tell me you haven't heard?" This was new. Diane and Misty always knew everything before me.

"Spill it," Misty replied.

"Amber tripped over a dead body on the Enchanted Trail last night. Vance and I heard her scream."

"What?" Diane shrieked, startling her costumers. She smiled politely when a dozen heads shot her way.

"And you didn't lead with that? You let me ramble on about someone breaking into my bookstore when we have another murder to solve?" Misty hissed.

"First off, the guy might've died of natural causes. Vance said he couldn't tell. Second, if not, it could all be related. Who knows." I shrugged.

"So this mystery man breaks into my bookstore and then is murdered on the Enchanted Trail? Somehow I can believe that."

"Or it's completely unrelated and some poor guy had a heart attack on the trail, and by coincidence, your bookstore was broken into last night," I countered. "Maybe it's a group of teenagers causing trouble? I have to admit that's what I thought when I heard about the high school," I confessed.

Misty seemed to think about it. "Maybe, but if it was vandalism, don't you think they would've damaged the inside of my store?"

"Not unless something scared them off?" Diane added before turning and walking away from us to wait on a customer.

"Anyway, how are you doing this morning?" Misty looked at me and forced a smile.

I was going to reply with something cheeky, like better than you, but my friend really did look rough. Instead, I answered honestly, "I'm tired but good. Vance stayed last night to help me finish those birdseed favors for the wedding and make sure I was okay."

"Birdseed?"

"You know, to toss at the bride and groom as they come out of the church."

"Won't it just go right through them?"

"You're bad." I laughed despite myself.

"What? It's true. They won't even have to flinch," Misty laughed. Then neither one of us could help it as we both cracked up. It was just the type of foolish comment to make us act like giggling school girls. There's nothing like laughter to help you release the tension you've been carrying around all week.

I cleared my throat after a moment. My eyes still crinkled in the corner from laughing. "Anyway, that's why I am here this morning. Eleanor asked me to pick out the cake."

"Because they can't eat it," Misty finished for me.

"Exactly."

"That is so sad. I'd hate not to be able to eat anymore." Misty looked longingly at the bakery case full of buttery, frosted goodness.

"I know." I copied her look and then snapped out of it. I couldn't do anything about ghosts not being able to eat anymore, but I could live my life here and now to the fullest. "Do you want a cupcake? Scratch that. I am buying you a cupcake."

"I haven't even had my coffee yet," Misty protested.

I gave her a pointed look. "Since when do you follow the rules? If anyone should be objecting, it should be me."

Misty pretended to wipe away a fake tear. "Look at you, becoming such a rulebreaker. After thirty years of friendship, I'm finally rubbing off on you."

"Heaven help us all," I quipped, and we found ourselves laughing again.

I went with a chocolate cupcake with ganache filling, and Misty went with a lemon cupcake with cream cheese frosting. We took our baked goods and cups of coffee and found an open table in the corner by the front window.

"I was going to grab a cup of coffee and come down and visit you like usual. I feel like we haven't had a chance to catch up yet," I said.

"I know. Vicki did a great job running things while I was gone, but there's so much I have to go over."

"So, how was it?" I couldn't imagine what it would be like being on tour with a rock star.

"It was amazing, truly. The energy, being in a packed arena with all those fans and the music? I loved it. It's addicting."

"Not to mention they're all chanting your boyfriend's name," I deadpanned.

"That definitely didn't hurt." Misty got a far-off expression. I felt like she was reliving a moment. Her eyes snapped back to me. "It's another world. I would jump on tour with him again in a heartbeat."

My eyebrows rose in surprise. "Really?" This was news. Misty generally liked to stay where she could control things.

"I know! I can't explain it. I told him I'd catch the end of the tour next month. I just had to make sure Vicki was good with it."

"And was she?"

Misty nodded. "I'll call Daniel in a little bit. Right now, I'm going to let him try and get some sleep."

Diane's bakery was a revolving door. I kept glancing up during our conversation and waving at the customers who walked in. "Good morning," I replied to Mrs. Potts, my second-grade teacher. Her arch-nemesis, Loretta Johnson, strolled in smugly after her. Mrs. Potts hesitated momentarily before holding the door open for her. It took a lot for Mrs. Potts to be rude, but Loretta Johnson had no problem strolling in front of her, not even bothering to utter a thank you.

"Well, I better head back to the store. Vicki's going to help me inventory everything and make sure nothing's missing."

"Good luck and I'm sorry again. Let me know if I can help somehow."

"You working this afternoon?"

"Yeah, at three. But I'm free this evening."

"Okay, I'll give you a call."

Misty had just left the bakery, and I had finished my cupcake when Eleanor and Percy floated inside. Eleanor's face beamed when she looked at me. She truly was a blushing bride. Percy, on the other hand, looked like he wanted to chuck a creampuff. Not because he was mad, but because the temptation was far too great. Mr. Skyler, the high school history teacher, had his face precariously close to his pastry while he bent low to blow into his coffee cup. I watched Percy eye the man. One flick of his wrist and the creampuff would be in the teacher's eye.

Percy smiled wickedly. I imagine the scene playing out in his head.

"Percy! Over here!" I snapped, getting the ghost's attention. I fought the urge to shake my finger at him. I grew up with the ghost. I knew his mind like I knew my own. Eleanor smiled, and Percy glowered as they came over to my table. "Are you ready to pick out your cake?"

"I'm thrilled." Eleanor clapped her hands together and looked about the space. While she eyed the cake display, I turned my attention to Percy. "Don't even think about it," I said under my breath.

"Who me?" But then he smiled.

"You are incorrigible. Your poor future wife."

"Nah, mischief keeps me young." Percy rubbed his hands together.

"Seriously, Percy. Don't ruin this for her."

Percy sobered instantly. "Well, when you put it that way." He mumbled, shoving his hands in his pockets.

The ghost floated over to his bride, and I made a mental note to pick up a bag of cream puffs on the way out. Percy could chuck them into the lake later if it would make him happy, or even at me if I was feeling adventurous. Besides, I could use a little practice with my deflecting charm, and what were friends for? I liked the new Percy, but I didn't want my favorite poltergeist to change too much.

Chapter 4

An hour later, we had the wedding cake all picked out, and I was ready to run to the office supply store to pick up the program stationary when Percy pulled me aside.

"Hey, Jelly," I looked at Percy suspiciously as soon as he used my childhood nickname. But instead of the teasing tone I was used to, Percy seemed unsure. Nervous even.

I didn't beat around the bush. "What's wrong?"

"Nothing's wrong," Percy drew out the last word. He gave a side glance at Eleanor, who was still talking to Diane. "It's just, I need to go pick up Eleanor's ring, and I wanted you to look at it. Tell me what you think?"

I exhaled, thankful that it really wasn't something worse. "I can do that. Do you want to go over right now?" Both the jeweler and Diane's bakery were located inside Village Square. The town's founders designed the outdoor storybook-style plaza so that everything could be reached on foot.

"Sure, I have a little bit of free time." That was a lie. I didn't have any free time, but this was obviously important to Percy, and I was happy to be there for him. I reminded myself to thank Eleanor once again for coming into his life and loving Percy for who he was. Because when a poltergeist got lonely or bored, look out.

Percy and I left shortly after waving our goodbyes and setting off to the jeweler. It was less than a ten-minute walk before we found ourselves at the front of the shopping plaza. My fingers latched onto the shop's handle, and I went to pull forward at the same time someone ran out. The man shoved the door with such force it sent me falling backward, tripping onto the sidewalk. My head scraped against the back of the building on my way down and hit the sidewalk, but the man didn't stop. He took off running for all his worth. I looked up through the haze of the pain radiating from the back of my head and saw that it was Harvey Johnson, Loretta's grandson. I was almost positive. Harvey wore his curly red hair tucked under a baseball cap, just like this man was now. It was his signature look.

"Jelly!" Percy hovered over me nervously.

I sat up slowly and squinted my eyes shut, willing the pain to subside. I may be a powerful witch, but I hadn't had much practice with healing spells. Something that I was going to have to remedy quickly. "That was Harvey Johnson, wasn't it?" My eyes winced.

"That's who that was! I knew I'd seen his face before. Wait till I get my hands on him. That boy will never have a restful night again as long as he lives."

It was sweet that the poltergeist was willing to haunt the man who had just practically knocked me out, but my mind was racing, wondering what set him out the door like a firecracker in the first place. I slowly rose and rubbed the back of my head. A bump was already beginning to form.

"Hey, what happened?" Vance jogged over to meet us.

I cracked open my eye. "Vance? What are you doing here?"

Vance opened and closed his mouth for a moment as if trying to come up with an excuse. He settled with, "Running errands. Now tell me what happened. You're hurt." Vance didn't say another word as he turned me around and began to examine the back of my head. I grimaced, biting my bottom lip as I bent my head forward. If it hurt this bad now, it would kill later this afternoon. But then, something magical began to happen. Vance held my head ever so gently. He placed one hand on my forehead, holding me in place while his other hand moved up the base of my neck. I couldn't make out the soft words of the incantation, but I shivered as the magic took hold. Coolness washed over me from the tips of his fingers. The back of my head began to tingle, numbing the pain. "Where did you learn how to do this?" My breath was a mere whisper as I felt relief come over me.

"I figured I should brush up on my healing spells with you at my side."

I wanted to reply with some witty retort but found myself thanking Vance instead. "Not going to lie. That's pretty smart of you."

When the spell was over, Vance turned me around to face him and held me in a tight hug to his chest. He kissed the top of my head and then pulled back, keeping me an arm's length away. "Now tell me who did this."

I swallowed, taking in Vance's fierce gaze. He wasn't usually so protective of me.

Percy answered before I couldn't find my voice. "It was Harvey Johnson. He came barreling out of the jewelry store and crashed right into Jelly. He didn't even stop!" Percy pointed to where we last saw Harvey.

Then, almost in slow motion, our group turned together and looked through the jewelry shop's front window.

Glass littered the floor, shining on the deep blue carpet like diamonds in the midmorning light. My expression turned to shock. "Harvey just robbed the jewelry store?" My second thought was, "Where's Katie?" She had taken over the store after Lyle passed away last year.

Vance wasted no time opening the door, "Katie!" he called out.

I was cognizant that this was a crime scene, but I couldn't stand at the threshold and wait for the sheriff if Katie was in trouble.

"Percy, can you search the back?" Ghosts didn't leave fingerprints, and he had a better chance of not disturbing the evidence.

"Katie?" I tried again, carefully stepping inside. Vance looked around the store, and together we headed slowly toward the side office, which also doubled as Katie's workshop. We were halfway down the hall when Percy caught up with us.

"Back here! She's in the storage closet, and it doesn't look too good."

My heart began to beat erratically in my chest. The adrenaline, which had begun to ebb, was back, pulsing in full force.

Vance jogged, closing the short distance, and I followed in his wake. Percy hadn't bothered to open the door. He walked right through the wall, so when Vance put his hand on the doorknob and twisted it open, Katie fell onto the floor. She was frozen solid.

"Oh my gosh, Katie!" I dropped down to my knees. Her entire body had frost on it. Her lips were blue, and her eyelashes were frosted. Thankfully, this was a spell that I knew. It was a freezing charm, one that I was quite fond of myself. Unlike the frost curse that hit our town a while back, Katie hadn't been turned into enchanted ice. We only needed to reverse the spell. I wasted no time withdrawing my wand. Vance did the same. I turned and looked up at him. "Tixi on three." Given how Katie was frozen solid, it would take all of my power and Vance's to thaw her.

I counted down, and Vance and I shouted the counter spell at the same time. A blue bolt of lightning shot forth from our wands and mixed together, hitting Katie solid in the chest. Within seconds, she was back. Her eyes blinked as she looked up and around the store, trying to figure out what had happened.

I leaned forward and helped to sit her up. "Are you okay?" I wasn't sure if Harvey had hit her with any other spells on his way out.

"What happened?" Katie struggled to stand, but her legs weren't working properly.

Vance met us on the ground. "Here, move slowly." He wrapped his arm around her back and helped her to her feet.

"I'm okay. Just confused." Together our group walked up the hallway into the store's display area.

"My store. What happened?" Tears filled Katie's eyes as she took in the destroyed display cases.

"I know, I'm sorry. We'll help you clean everything up." I rubbed Katie's shoulders.

"What's the last thing you remember?" Vance gently prodded.

Katie closed her eyes and shook her head as if trying to will the memories to resurface.

Her eyes fixed off into the distance. "I remember opening the store." She paused while she thought about it. "I went to the back to go to the safe to get out a ring." Katie looked at Vance. If I hadn't been staring, I wouldn't have caught the questioning look they shared. I wasn't sure what that was about, but Vance encouraged her to continue. Katie swallowed nervously. "That's it. That's all I remember. One minute my hand was on the safe's dial, and the next, I'm looking up at you."

"We need to check the safe," Vance said, his voice holding a bit of an edge to it.

"It's empty!" Percy sang back.

"What?" Vance practically growled.

"No! All my inventory's in there. All those loose gems. My custom pieces. Who would do this?"

"It was Harvey Johnson. He ran into me on the way out," I answered.

"I'm calling the sheriff, now." Vance had his cell phone out and was dialing the number in seconds.

"It'll be okay. Don't worry," I tried to reassure Katie. Harvey had certainly made off with a small fortune, but we knew where he lived. I doubt he could make it far before the sheriff caught up with him.

My mind immediately jumped to Misty's store, and I wondered if Harvey had been the one to break in there as well. In theory, it made sense. I mean, how many burglars did we have running around Silverlake? But the jewelry store had been a smash and grab job, whereas the bookstore had been what? A break-in with no entering? Unless Diane's theory was correct: Harvey planned to steal the cash register, but he got spooked. I'd make sure to mention the bookstore to whatever deputy arrived on the scene.

I WAS happy to see it was Deputy Jones who answered the call. It didn't take long for him to take our statements and let us go. Have I mentioned how much I wished he could be the sheriff? I did, truly. It was fortunate we had at least one deputy who had a solid head on his shoulders. You could always count on Deputy Jones to do the right thing and not follow the sheriff around, nipping at his heels like the rest of the department.

"When you find Harvey, don't forget to ask about the bookstore," I reminded the deputy as I walked out the door.

Vance and I parted ways at the jewelry store

after I promised him I was feeling much better. My head no longer hurt. Vance headed to his office and planned to keep an ear out for when they brought Harvey in, and I planned to finally pick up that stationary and get back to work on the wedding programs.

I was hoping to have an hour to print them out and fold them before clocking in. The programs Eleanor picked out matched the birdseed favors, meaning they were both accented with the same ribbon. I was already dreading working with the material.

"Call me as soon as you get the all-clear, and I'll come over and help you clean up," I told Katie on my way out.

She nodded that she heard me but went back to talking to Deputy Jones immediately.

I made a mental note to stop by Connie's and pick up a calming tonic for Katie. Maybe two. After the last twenty-four hours, we both needed one.

Chapter 5

My afternoon didn't go as planned. With the way my morning had started, I shouldn't have been surprised, but still, it would've been nice if the pearlized paper would've fed seamlessly through the laser printer. After trying every printing trick I knew, including hand-feeding the paper sheet by sheet, I was ready to give up. I eyed the printer, wanting to curse it a thousand different ways or maybe chuck it right into the lake when Vance called me. I needed the distraction.

"Hey, how's it going?" I said on an exhale. I hated to admit I was a little out of breath. The printer had turned out to be a worthy opponent.

"Is this a bad time?" I could tell I'd piqued Vance's curiosity based on his inflection.

"No, I just went head-to-head with the printer.

Don't ask." I could picture Vance opening his mouth to follow up with a question, only to shut it.

"Okay..." He pivoted the conversation. "Listen, I was calling to tell you Deputy Jones brought Harvey in. He found him at his buddy's house. You know that Derek Sawyer guy?"

"Those two are inseparable." I wasn't surprised he was involved at all.

"Deputy Jones said they both ran when they saw him, but Harvey tripped, and that's how the deputy caught up with him. He planned on playing good cop until diamonds rained down on the ground."

"I knew it was him," I shook my head. What an idiot. "What was he thinking?"

"I don't know. The sheriff's questioning him right now."

"You know Loretta's going to call you and ask you to represent him."

"You're probably right, but I don't know if I want the case. Have you seen the guy's rap sheet? He's been charged with check fraud, insurance fraud, and pickpocketing. Any illegal way to make money."

"I knew he had gotten into trouble, but I didn't know how extensive it was."

"Half the charges are from out of state. Pretty sure that's why he's living here again."

"He's hiding out."

"I know we don't have all the evidence, but if I

was his lawyer and it was as bad as it looked, I'd recommend a plea deal if he could get one. Maybe he wasn't the only man in on the job."

"You make a good point. I wonder if Harvey was working alone?"

"Hopefully, the sheriff will find out."

"Have you heard anything about the mystery man on the trail?" I kept my voice light, but inside I was dying to know more.

"Nothing. The sheriff's kept a tight lid on it. It's not even in the paper."

"Huh."

"Do you still have wedding stuff to do tonight?" It took me a second to catch up when Vance changed the subject.

I thought of the printer and gave it the stink eye. "Unfortunately." Even if I didn't get the printer to work, I still had plenty to do.

"Do you want me to pick up takeout and come over to you?"

"You don't have to. I'm sure there's something else you'd rather be doing—"

Vance cut me off. "I honestly just want to spend time with you."

Whatever I was going to say was forgotten. What woman could argue with that?

"I want to spend time with you, too," I confessed. "I'm at the desk until seven, so sometime after that?"

"Seven thirty it is. I'll see you in a little bit. Don't work too hard."

"You either."

It wasn't even an hour later when I snapped my head up, expecting to check in a new guest, when I came face-to-face with Loretta Johnson herself. "Loretta, what can I do for you?"

Loretta's eyes darted around the lobby. The lobby was pretty empty in the summertime as people tended to get outside and explore versus staying in and cozying up in front of the fire. After ensuring we were alone, Loretta leaned forward and said, "I need your help."

"My help?" I had no idea how I could help Loretta.

"You need to prove that Harvey's innocent."

"Loretta," I couldn't hide the exasperation from my voice. "He ran right into me at the crime scene and knocked me down. I probably would have a concussion if Vance hadn't shown up moments later."

It was as if Loretta hadn't heard a single word I'd said. "He was set up. He had to be. That's what he told me, and I believe him." Loretta tapped a polished red fingernail on my registration desk as she continued to insist on her grandson's innocence.

"I don't see how I can help, though. I think you should call a lawyer. Someone like Vance." After our earlier conversation, I doubted Vance would even take the case. Still, it seemed like the right thing to do was to refer Loretta to an actual attorney and not someone who pretended to be a legal assistant every so often.

"I don't want Vance. I want you. You're good at this sort of thing. How many cases have you solved?" It was a rhetorical question. Technically, the answer was five, but I kept that number to myself. "Just talk to him, please. Sheriff Reynolds said I'm allowed to visit him."

That comment took me back. "He did?" The sheriff never offered anything.

"I may have threatened to call his mama." Loretta looked innocently down at her nails before looking back up at me. I almost flinched at the raw emotions playing across her face. "I need your help, Angelica. Come down and talk with him, and if after you do, you still think he's guilty, then I'll call Vance."

I felt a headache building between my eyes. There wasn't a single ounce of me that believed Harvey was innocent. A man doesn't tear out of a jewelry store and knock a woman down if he's a model of honesty. But I also couldn't look Loretta in the eyes and tell her no. Sometimes it was easier to say yes.

As much as Loretta wanted me to drop everything and follow her to the sheriff's department right that second, she had to wait until I had coverage for the front desk, which would take a couple of hours. That time flew by as I checked guests in, recommended the best local restaurants, gave walking directions to our iconic witch fountain at Wishing Well Park, weighed in on the average time it took to walk around the lake, and reminded guests what time canoe rentals ended.

I shouldn't have been surprised when Loretta showed up in the lobby two hours later, right on the dot.

"Are you ready?" The older woman had pulled her dyed chestnut brown locks up into a twist and wore a red pantsuit. She eyed me skeptically. I looked down at my jeans and T-shirt. If she thought I was copying her and dressing up in a lawyer, power-vibe outfit, she was mistaken.

"I'll meet you there," I said, retrieving my keys from the back. When Aunt Thelma was in town, we shared a car, but she had left it with me when she went to Mount Holly, insisting she didn't need it. "Everyone rides around in sleighs!" I later discovered cars weren't even allowed in the Christmas village, which sounded magical and charming, and everything an enchanted Christmas village should be.

Loretta looked disappointed we wouldn't be riding together, but I wanted to ensure I wasn't at her mercy. Plus, I needed to call Vance on my way. I purposely hadn't called after Loretta left, giving him a chance to get some work done. I knew he had hundreds of emails to go through from being out of the office. Vance was a lot like me, liking to be caught up with work as soon as possible. Neither of us liked to admit it, but we could both be workaholics. It was a character flaw we were aware of, which was why Vance's confession of wanting to spend time with me was extra sweet.

Vance answered his phone after a few rings.

"Hey, do you want to meet up for dinner instead?" I asked.

"That's fine. Is everything okay?"

"For the most part. Loretta showed up at the inn and asked me to talk with Harvey. She's convinced he's innocent and has been set up. She thinks I can help somehow."

"Wow. You're headed there now?"

"Yeah. I told Loretta she should talk to you, but she wants me to have a go with Harvey first. Personally, I think she's in denial, but who knows, maybe I'll get some good information out of him."

"Okay, well give me a call when you're done, and we can meet up."

"You got it. Love you. See you soon."

"Love you too."

I clicked off with Vance and drove the rest of the way to the sheriff's department in silence, unsure what Harvey could possibly say to sway me to his side.

When I pulled into the sheriff's department, Loretta practically blocked me in with her car, pulling up behind me. I don't know what she thought I was going to do. Change my mind and burn rubber out of there? It wasn't until I parked and got out of the car that Loretta readjusted her car and pulled up alongside me.

"Sheriff Reynolds said he'll give us five minutes, and you can bet I'll make sure he gives us at least that." Loretta marched up the steps beside me. When we walked inside, I gave the receptionist, Dottie, a wave and said hello. Dottie was new to town. The jury was still out as to whether she would be Team Sheriff Reynolds or Team Deputy Jones. In other words, would she be an asset or an obstacle? Only time would tell. For now, we were friendly with one another.

"Oh, Angelica?" Dottie said as we passed by.

"Yeah?" I stopped walking and turned to face the woman.

"I was wondering what type of availability you had at the inn next weekend. My family's decided to come into town last minute and see my new place." Dottie blushed. I wasn't sure if it was because her family was an embarrassment or if she was simply flushed with excitement at their upcoming visit.

I mentally pulled up the reservation log. We had more rooms open than I'd like to admit. "You should be good, but I recommend making reservations soon to be on the safe side."

"Oooh, okay. Thanks, I will."

"Mrs. Johnson, you're right on time." Sheriff Reynolds strolled toward the reception area. His brow furrowed when he took in my appearance. "And I see you brought Ms. Nightingale with you. Do you need to amend your statement?" The sheriff eyed me suspiciously as if Loretta had convinced me to lie about what had happened.

"No, I stand by what I said. Harvey Johnson ran me down fleeing the jewelry store."

Loretta scoffed. "Well, I'm sure even if that's true, he had a good reason."

Yeah, he had just robbed the place, I thought.

"You said we could talk with him. Where is he?" Loretta continued, unaware of my thoughts.

"At the end of the hall, first door on your left. You've got five minutes."

I didn't need any further direction. I had been in the first door on the left plenty of times. I hesitated briefly before tugging the door handle down and pushing the heavy metal door in.

Harvey was zoned out, his gaze fixed on the floor when we entered.

"Grandma?" Harvey looked surprised to see Loretta. His gaze then flicked over to me. "Who's she?"

"It's Angelica Nightingale. Don't you remember? She can home and lives at Mystic Inn with her aunt. You should be happy to see her." Harvey looked skeptical. "Wipe that look off your face. You've gotten yourself in a world of trouble, boy. I asked Angelica to come down here and straighten this all out. She's good with puzzles like this."

Harvey sat back in his chair and assessed me. I was doing the same, trying to get a feel for his thoughts. "I suppose it won't hurt talking to you. I don't know what else to do." Harvey shook his head and looked defeated.

I pulled back the metal chair along the linoleum floor and sat across from him. Loretta took up her post in the corner of the room, sitting in the only remaining chair.

"Your grandma seems to think you're innocent," I started off by saying.

"I am." Harvey raised his voice along with his chin. "Someone set me up." The expression dared me to call him out on it.

I tried to keep my expression neutral but failed miserably. My head cocked to the side as if to say, *C'mon.*

"If you don't believe me, what are you even doing here?" Harvey looked over to his grandma. "I thought you said she was here to help."

"Listen, Harvey. You barreled into me fleeing the jewelry store. I smacked my head on the way down. I'm lucky I have friends who know how to heal."

Harvey looked at me and swallowed uncomfortably. "I did? Honestly, I don't remember." Harvey's eyes were wide as panic washed over him. "I swear to you. It was an accident. I didn't do it on purpose. I was trying to get out of there."

"Because you robbed the store?"

"No! Man, I already told you I didn't do it!" Harvey rubbed his hand down his face in exasperation. "There's a hole in my head. A big one. It sucked my memory right out with it."

"You're missing part of your memory?" I looked over to Loretta to see what she thought of that statement, but her eyes were trained on Harvey.

"I just said that didn't I?" Harvey pushed back from the table. Agitation pulsed off of him.

I decided I better try a different tack. "Okay, why don't we back up and you tell me what you remember. Do you remember going to the jewelry store?"

"Nuh-uh. All I remember is waking up in the hallway. My head hurt really bad. Then I saw all that broken glass, and I bolted. I knew it didn't look good. I've done some stupid things, but I don't mess with grand theft. Swear to you."

"What about the diamonds? They found them in your pocket."

"I didn't put them there. I'm not stupid. If I

robbed a store, I wouldn't keep the goods on me. I'm telling you, someone set me up."

"Why, though? Who would want to do that to you?"

Harvey wouldn't meet my gaze. "I don't know," he lied.

"Harvey, look at me." His eyes drifted over, but he wouldn't maintain contact. "I'm going to be honest. Your defense is weak. If you don't give me a name, something to go off of, I can't help you."

Harvey was silent as the seconds ticked by.

Loretta spoke up from the corner. "You have to trust her, Harvey."

"I don't need your help, all right!" Harvey scraped the legs of his chair across the floor and abruptly stood up. Frustration rolled off of him in waves. Whatever was going through his mind, he wasn't willing to share it with us.

Sheriff Reynolds walked through the door at that moment, not even bothering to knock. "Time's up, ladies. I'm going to have to ask you two to step outside."

I nodded to the sheriff. Harvey continued to pace, looking agitated. Loretta walked over to her grandson. I didn't wait to hear what she said. Instead, I saw myself out of the room.

"What did you find out?" Deputy Jones met me in the hallway.

"He's not telling us everything he knows." He

might've been set up. Had his memory erased, even. But the man also knew who was behind it. I'd bet my wand on it. "Do you think it might all be connected?"

"What do you mean?"

"The jewelry robbery. The break-in at the bookstore. The dead man on the Enchanted Trail." I ticked the items off on my fingers.

"The jewelry store and bookstore wouldn't surprise me, but I don't think the man on the trail is connected."

"Did you ID him?"

Deputy Jones looked around before answering. "We did. Haven't connected with his next of kin yet, so we're not releasing a statement yet."

I nodded. "I understand. I only wanted to mention the possibility."

"Believe me, I know. I thought of it too. But it looks like Harvey is our bad guy for the jewelry store at least."

"Yeah, you're probably right." But there was more to it. I was sure of it.

Chapter 6

Vance and I met up at the tavern. There'd be plenty of time in the future for romantic dinners and glasses of red wine. But right then, we both wanted a good burger and a cold beer. Plus, the tavern felt comfortable. I waved to Bonnie, who owned the place with her husband, as I made my way to meet Vance in what had quickly become our booth. If it was open, you could bet that's where we sat. Vance stood up, sliding out from his side, and greeted me with a kiss on the cheek.

"Your day go okay?" he asked as we both took our seats.

"Eh, it was okay. Yours?"

"About the same."

Bonnie came over then to take our order. Neither one of us needed to look at a menu. I went with a smokehouse burger with extra barbecue sauce and onion rings, and Vance went with a black and blue burger, extra blue cheese.

"Two tall drafts?" Bonnie asked before we could add a drink order.

We both agreed. Bonnie turned and shouted something over her shoulder at the other bartender, holding up two fingers. "I'll be right back with those."

"So, what did Harvey say?" Vance said as we awaited our drinks.

I went ahead and filled him in.

"Do you think he was set up?" Vance asked when I finished recapping the visit.

I thought before answering. "I'm not sure. Harvey seemed believable, but he's not telling us everything. He wouldn't say who was behind it, but he knows. I wish I knew more about the mystery man. I'd like to know if he plays into this at all."

"Agree."

"I guess for now I'm back to thinking the robberies are connected and wondering who Harvey's working with."

"Like a business partner?"

"Maybe." I could see that.

"They could've been working together, and then the other guy turned on him and hit him with a spell."

I clucked my tongue on the roof of my mouth while I thought.

"Maybe it's his friend Derek? Although why you'd run back to the guy who'd just cursed you is beyond me."

"Unless Harvey doesn't remember he cursed him," Vance countered.

"Hmmm, we should probably pay Derek a visit."

"But not tonight," Vance added.

"No, not tonight."

Bonnie set our drafts down in front of us. We stopped our conversation to thank her. I took a sip of my drink. The cold draft felt good going down my throat. My stomach rumbled, hoping the burger and onion rings wouldn't be too far behind.

Vance opened his mouth to say something when he was interrupted by Mrs. Potts. I hadn't realized the retiree was sitting in the booth behind us, readily able to hear our conversation.

"I don't mean to eavesdrop, but I have to tell you, stay out of this Harvey Johnson business." Before I could get a word in, Mrs. Potts continued, "That boy is a no-good scoundrel. He's a conman too. You can't trust him or that grandmother of his."

Vance spoke up first. "How well do you know Harvey?"

"As long as I've known Loretta, so too long.

One summer, I tried to give Harvey the benefit of the doubt. He gave me some sob story about trying to earn money to go to mechanic school. I gave in and paid him to paint my shutters. Do you think he ever did? No, he took the money and ran."

"That's awful. Did you ever get it back?" I asked.

"Oh, I did, but it wasn't easy. Loretta made up a dozen excuses why he couldn't stop by this day or that. Eventually, I got tired of waiting. Mike McCormick came over and did it for free! After the job was done, Loretta couldn't spin any more stories. She had to pay me back. Doubt the boy ever gave her a penny."

"At least you got your money back," I replied.

"I may have gotten my money back, but more than that, I learned a lesson—you don't trust Harvey Johnson. Mark my words: you'll regret helping him if you do." Mrs. Potts looked solemnly at me.

I nodded. "Thanks for telling us your story."

"Least I could do. I hate to see good people get taken advantage of. Us good folks have to look out for one another."

"We appreciate that," Vance added.

"Guess I'll leave you two to enjoy your dinner." Mrs. Potts waved over her shoulder and said farewell.

She left the tavern right after. Vance waited until

she was out of earshot before saying, "I don't know, maybe she's right."

"You think I should stay out of it?"

"I think you can't trust Harvey."

"Trust me. I'd already figured that one out on my own."

I managed to make it a whopping fifteen hours without talking about Harvey Johnson. I called Katie after dinner to see if she needed any help cleaning up the store, but she never got back with me, and it was locked up tight when Vance and I swung by.

It wasn't until the next morning, when I was working behind the registration desk bright and early, that Harvey came slamming back to the forefront of my thoughts. Misty came whirling into Mystic Inn. She was dressed in chic casual from her shiny, dark, styled locks and designer sunglasses down to her lightly faded denim cutoffs and bright white sneakers.

"What are you doing here?" Since dating Daniel, Misty was no longer a morning person. It must have something to do with all those late, post-concert nights. Add the fact that she was not only here right now but looking fabulous? You could say my curiosity was piqued.

"Remember how I said I would hop back on tour with Daniel in a heartbeat? Well, he called last night and convinced me to come back. He has three sold-out shows in LA, and you know how I love me some California sun." Misty beamed.

"That I do," I smiled at my friend. She was so blissfully happy that it was impossible not to.

"Anyway, before I head out to catch my flight, I wanted to ask if you mind checking in with Vicki for me? She says she can handle everything, but I want to make sure she's not just saying that. If you go in and she looks super stressed out or something, promise you'll call me?"

"I promise. I'll stop by later today."

"Thank you." Misty's smile faltered. "I'd feel even better if we knew who was behind all these break-ins. I'd hate to leave and have the bookstore broken into again."

"I did bring that up to Deputy Jones. Maybe Harvey is behind both? I meant to ask him, but I forgot yesterday." Misty cocked her head, reminding me that I hadn't told her about visiting Harvey. "Loretta asked me to go down and talk to Harvey because she's convinced he's innocent and thinks I can help prove it. But I don't know. He might've not acted alone, but I'm sure he had something to do with it."

"You haven't heard?"

"Haven't heard what?"

"Harvey was turned to stone last night."

"What?"

"Loretta found him just before dinner."

"Wait, back up. The sheriff released him?"

"Not like that. The sheriff did end up charging Harvey for the burglary. After he was arraigned, Loretta paid his bail, and they went home. A couple of hours later, Loretta went to check on him and found him in his bed, hard as concrete. No witnesses, either."

I was dumbfounded. "Is he dead?"

"Not as far as I know. Vicki's the one who told me all of this. She heard from Diane when she went to pick us up some coffee. Rumor has it, it's a gargoyle charm and a strong one. Regular sunlight spells don't seem to be working."

I was silent for a moment. "You know what this means?" Misty looked at me expectantly. "Harvey was telling the truth. At least partially."

"And someone wants to keep him quiet." Misty gave me a leveled stare.

"I knew he wasn't being completely honest with me yesterday. I'm betting whoever set him up is the same person who cursed him, worried he would talk."

"I wonder who that person is?"

"Me too." If Loretta were determined to prove her grandson's innocence before, she'd be downright obsessed now. I imagined she'd be visiting me sometime soon. I still wasn't sure how much I wanted to get involved.

Misty looked down at her phone. I could tell she had to get going, yet she stayed rooted to the spot.

"Don't you have a flight to catch?"

"I do, but I hate leaving the town like this. What if more people turn to stone? What if more shops get robbed? What if that mystery guy was murdered? It's not right for me to take off, living in some fantasy world, while everything here is falling apart."

"Everything is not falling apart. The sheriff will figure it out."

"You mean you'll figure it out. You always do. The sheriff should put you on the payroll."

"Yeah, that's never going to happen. And I wouldn't want him to either."

"What do you mean? You put in the work."

I held up my finger to silence Misty, "But then I'd have to answer to the sheriff." I made a stink face.

"Oh, good point. Yeah, forget the money then."

"My thoughts exactly."

Misty's bubbly excitement began to pop as she

continued to think about Silverlake and what might happen while she was gone.

"Maybe I should cancel." Misty twisted her lips as she thought about it.

"Nope, none of that. You are going to LA and having a blast. I promise I will take care of this."

"I thought you were going to stay out of it?"

"That's before my best friend thought about canceling her flight. Besides, I'm a business owner in this town, too. It's in my best interest to figure out who the thief is and make sure Silverlake is safe." My mind thought back to the black cat rummaging around outside two nights before. It might be nothing, or it might be a fellow witch casing my property. Regardless, the more I thought about it, the more I was determined to get to the bottom of this case.

Chapter 8

I wasted no time heading out after Emily came in to take over for me. I told her and Percy to give me a call if they had any questions or needed any help. My first stop was Loretta's house. I wanted to check out the scene of the crime and see what else Loretta could tell me. I had been to Loretta's house before. Last time, my aunt's best friend Clemmie had me tag along undercover to their magical cooking club meeting. Who knew I would be back investigating another case so soon.

When I pulled onto Loretta's street, I held back, recognizing the sheriff's cruiser in her driveway. I debated if I should drive by and come back later when I saw the cruiser's brake lights flash, and the vehicle started to roll down the driveway. I put my car into drive instead of idling on the side of the road, cruising past Loretta's house. I planned on hanging out one street over until I knew the sheriff was well on his way. I sat pulled over on the side of the road, scrolling through my phone for a minute when a knock came on my passenger side window.

The noise caused my shoulders to flinch. Speak of the devil. Clemmie waved, telling me to roll down the window.

"I was just thinking about you," I confessed. I hadn't seen Clemmie as much now that my aunt was dividing her time between Silverlake and Mount Holly.

"You were? Isn't that sweet."

"How have you been?"

From the looks of it, Clemmie was out for a power walk. She wore a white sun visor, a purple tank top, and athletic shorts. She held small hand weights, probably nothing more than two pounds each.

"Good, good. Listen, are you working the Harvey case?"

Clemmie's bluntness did not surprise me. "I'm trying to. Waiting on the sheriff to leave. Why, what have you heard?"

Clemmie leaned in closer. "You know I don't mind spilling the tea, but I don't want it getting traced back to me." The idiom was appropriate, seeing Clemmie owned a tea shop.

"Go on."

"I was out for a morning walk last week, and I

heard Loretta and Harvey fighting. They must've been outside in the backyard, but their voices carried. Anyway, she told him he needed to take on some responsibility. That he was a grown man now," Clemmie used air quotes, "and it was time that he started acting like one."

"Interesting. I was under the impression Loretta always bailed Harvey out."

"She always has, and I think she's tired of it."

"I don't blame her."

"Not that she'll ever admit that to anyone. I couldn't hear everything, but Harvey said something about getting money to pay her back, but I kept on walking and didn't think anything of it until I heard he robbed that jewelry store. How are you feeling, by the way?" Clemmie's eyes filled with concern as she assessed me through the window.

"Fine, better than fine, really. Vance showed up and healed me with a charm." I absentmindedly rubbed the back of my head where I had hit the building.

"I've always liked Vance. Even when you two had that falling out. There's something special about him. He's a good one."

I tried not to laugh at Clemmie's definition of a falling out. I didn't speak to Vance for thirteen years, and I never would have again if my aunt hadn't tricked me into coming home.

"I better let you get back to it." Clemmie tapped

the window frame. "If you need any help, you know who to call."

"Thank you. You know I'll take you up on it."

"And you know I'm hoping you will." Clemmie winked and then turned and walked away, pumping the weights with each step. I shook my head and smiled at the image and then put my car into drive and pulled away from the curb.

Loretta's driveway was empty when I returned. Regardless, I skipped parking in that space in case someone else stopped by and blocked me in. Loretta's garage door opened as I walked up the driveway. Loretta stood at the entrance with her car keys in hand.

"Angelica? I was just on my way to see you."

I wasn't surprised. I knew Loretta would be back asking for my help. "I beat you to it."

"Does this mean you'll take on the case?"

"I don't know about anything as formal as that." It wasn't like I was a licensed private investigator, "But I'm here to help in any way that I can."

Up close, I could tell Loretta had been crying. Her eyes were red-rimmed, and her complexion was blotchy.

"Thank you so much. I know if anyone can get to the bottom of this, you can. Here, come inside and let me put on some coffee." I followed Loretta into her well-kept kitchen. Her countertops were gleaming in the morning light, and her appliances were streak-free. It was the type of kitchen that looked like no one ever cooked in it, but if you knew Loretta, you knew she was simply a perfectionist. Loretta motioned to the small kitchen table. An oversized window framed the space, providing a lovely view of Loretta's rose garden. Loretta joined me, carrying a cake plate topped with scones in one hand and a cup of coffee in the other. She made one more trip for her coffee and the cream and sugar set.

The dine-in kitchen area was warm and cozy with the mint-green painted walls, white cupboards, and gray quartz countertops. I had a feeling Loretta took most of her meals here versus the formal dining room through the other side of the archway.

"Thank you so much for this. You don't have to wait on me."

"Nonsense, having you here to fuss over almost makes me feel normal."

I could understand that. I didn't know Loretta that well, but I knew I'd feel the same if I were in her shoes. If I was being honest, my opinion of Loretta was prejudiced from everything Mrs. Potts had said. But the truth was, I hadn't spent enough time around Loretta to truly know her. I decided to try to have an open mind. "Why don't you tell me what happened last night?" I tore off a chunk of the scone and popped it in my mouth. The flavor burst with lemon and sugar. It was so good. There was a reason why Loretta was one of the founding members of the Simmering Sisters cooking club. The woman knew her way around a kitchen. Adding a dash of magic to her recipes never hurt either.

"We got back here around seven. Harvey went down to his room, and I told him I'd see to super, vegetable soup and French bread." Loretta added as if that detail was important. "When it was ready, I went downstairs to tell him, and that's when I found him." A tear leaked from the corner of Loretta's eye and slid down her cheek. She stood and fetched a tissue from the kitchen counter. "I'm sorry. I'm not usually such a leaky watering pot. In my heart, I know Harvey will be all right. We'll reverse the spell. But then what? Is he going to end up in jail for a crime he didn't commit?"

"About that. Do you think Harvey could've been involved somehow? Like maybe he was in on it, but then the friend turned on him?"

Loretta stared at me and blinked as if she couldn't believe I had just suggested such a thing. "Harvey is innocent. He wasn't involved in this one bit," she snapped back.

I took a sip of my coffee to buy myself some time. I wondered if Loretta believed that or if she couldn't admit the truth. I decided it didn't matter. I would be better off looking for clues.

I shifted tactics. "Can I see his room?"

"If you think it might help." Loretta seemed unsure but slid her chair back and stood, leading the way. I quickly followed. Loretta opened the door off the kitchen leading downstairs. She flipped the switch on the way down. Overhead fluorescent lighting flicked to life from the dropdown ceiling. Loretta's basement wasn't like a newly built home with drywall, carpeting, and ample daylight. No, this basement was stacked cinder blocks with a concrete floor and two slivers for windows. One side of the room housed an extra refrigerator and Loretta's washer and dryer units. The other half of the room was dominated by Harvey's bed, a tall chest of drawers, and heaven only knew what else. Harvey had thrown his dirty clothes and sheets on the floor. He'd left an open jar of peanut butter on the bedside table, balanced on a stack of magazines. I stepped over random car parts—at least that's what I thought they were—as I took in the space.

"I'm sorry about the mess." Loretta blushed a deep scarlet. "It kills me to let him live this way, but I won't pick up after him anymore."

"That's understandable." Harvey was a man well into his twenties. He shouldn't need his grandmother cleaning up after him. The only problem was, with the room being such a mess, it was impossible to know a clue when you saw one.

"What are you looking for exactly?" Loretta seemed to read my mind.

"I'm not sure. I was hoping to recognize it when I saw it." I mentally went through a list of spells and charms that I knew to see if one might help. Ideally, I would use a summoning charm, but those only worked if you know what you were looking for. Since I had no idea what I was looking for, it didn't matter how powerful I was. I wouldn't be able to call the item to me. "We need to find something that will tie Harvey to whoever set him up." Loretta perked up at my statement. I wanted to say whoever *might* have set him up, but I knew Loretta would be less likely to help if she still thought I doubted her grandson's innocence.

"The sheriff already went through his things."

"Did he find anything?"

"Not that I'm aware of."

If I knew the sheriff, he hadn't looked too hard. While we stood together in the space, I thought of another question for Loretta. "How do you think the attacker got in? Did you hear anything?" I looked back up at the windows. They were at ground level to the outside. Plastic, dome-shaped molds covered the top of the window wells, dimming the already minimal natural light.

It was hard to imagine someone had managed to take off the plastic window coverings, fit through the window, and curse Harvey without Loretta noticing. I then wondered if the person could have done the spell through the window. But even that was risky. The magic could've bounced off the glass and come back at them.

"Sheriff Reynolds asked me the same thing. After making the soup, I let it simmer for about a half hour and went to take a bath to relax. I assume it must have happened then."

"Was your door unlocked?"

"Not the front door, but the back one was. That's normal for when we're home here. I often go in and out, reading out back or weeding my flowers."

I nodded, "You're probably right then." I didn't want to add that the bad guy had probably been watching Loretta, waiting to make his move.

My eyes scanned the room, taking in Harvey's personal artifacts which consisted mostly of car posters and magazines. I didn't see any electronics, not even a television. "Does Harvey have a cell phone or computer?"

"He has a cell phone, but the sheriff took it."

"No TV or computer?"

"Oh no, what would he need those for?"

"Just curious." I filed that information away for later. The sheriff wouldn't let me access Harvey's contact log, but Deputy Jones might if I asked him nicely enough.

"What about valuables? Does Harvey keep them someplace special?" I moved towards the tall dresser and slid open the first drawer. I expected to find socks and underwear or maybe even T-shirts. Instead, I found stacks of baseball cards, a couple of packs of cigarettes, dozens of receipts, a few pocketknives, two belt buckles, a handful of lighters, and an expired driver's license.

"Mind if I take a picture of his ID? The picture might help."

"His what?"

"Driver's license?" I held the rectangular card up. It had expired two years ago. "Unless you have a more recent picture?"

Loretta took the identification from me and scanned it. She scowled. "I sure hope he renewed it."

I shrugged. I had no idea.

"No, I suppose I don't mind." She handed the card back.

I took out my cell phone and snapped a picture of it, focusing on the image and not the personal details.

"You know, now that I think about it, when Harvey was a little boy, he used to keep his money in his pillowcase. I still find a couple of trinkets now and then. Things he won while playing poker. He'd keep them for a bit and then pawn them off." Loretta motioned to the bed.

I reached for Harvey's pillow, shaking the first one out, and came up empty. The second one was the same. It wasn't until I tugged out the third one, wedged between the headboard and the wall, that I found something noteworthy. A silver ring with an opal flanked by two smaller diamonds plopped out onto the bed. "You mean something like this?" I was careful not to touch the ring and get my prints on it. Instead, I took my cell phone out and snapped a few pics of it.

"That's beautiful," Loretta leaned forward and remarked.

"You might want to call the sheriff back and tell him what you found." Loretta hesitated, and I knew she had no intention of telling the sheriff anything about the ring. For all she knew, the ring belonged to the jewelry store, and the piece was only more evidence stacked against her grandson.

I didn't see a point in wasting more time searching the room. Instead, I asked Loretta if she would mind cleaning it up and letting me know if she found anything.

"Maybe a note or a name and phone number?" I suggested

"I can do that. This mess is driving me crazy anyway."

"I know Harvey hangs out with Derek a lot. Is there anyone else I should talk to?"

"No, just pretty much him. I'm not sure if Derek's around right now. He's been taking care of family over in Rincon." Loretta thought for a moment. "But you know what, Harvey did have a job last week. He helped clean out the old Craddock house after Michael passed away. I forgot about that."

"Did the family hire him?" I remembered seeing people coming and going from the Craddock house when I'd driven by last week, but I didn't remember seeing Harvey. Not that I'd been paying that much attention.

"You know, I'm not sure. He works a couple different jobs. I know Harvey said it paid real well."

"Thanks for that. I'll check with them." I followed Loretta back up the stairs. In the kitchen, I blinked a time or two, letting my eyes readjust to the abundant, bright light.

"If you think of any more questions, here's my cell phone number. Give me a call. I don't care what time it is." Loretta tore off a piece of paper from the pad she kept by the phone and jotted down her number. She folded the paper and handed it over. I readily took it, pocketed it, and turned to leave. "Oh, one more thing. Do you know where Derek lives?"

Loretta scrunched her nose. "The Crossroads. Bright orange trailer. You can't miss it."

"Ah." Loretta didn't have to say anymore. The Crossroads was a unique magical community. One that shunned the happy-go-lucky tourist vibe of Silverlake and preferred to be their own gritty coven of misfits and outcasts. They weren't all witches either, a majority were shifters cast out of their packs. I'd only been out to The Crossroads one time in high school for a party. I thought I was acting cool. It turned out I was being stupid. Aunt Thelma threatened to transfigure me permanently into a cat if she ever heard I went out there again. I told her she had nothing to worry about. The place gave me the heebie jeebies. The entire time I was there, I felt invisible eyes on me. We were outside at a bonfire. I swore something was stalking me from the surrounding corn fields, watching and waiting for me to separate from the group so it could attack. At first, I thought the air was only thick with smoke, but it was more than that. Magic crackled in the atmosphere. The entire community felt like one big pressure cooker. One wrong move and the entire thing would explode. I chalked it up to too much ungrounded energy and raw shifter power. And now there was a chance I'd need to drive out there again? I can tell you one thing, it wasn't a trip I'd make alone.

Chapter 9

I was going to wait for Vance before heading out to The Crossroads. I thought it would be smart to have someone with me to watch my back. Good thing Aunt Thelma wasn't in town. She'd probably still forbid me from going there.

I might have to wait to visit the shady community, but I didn't have to wait to swing by the Craddock house. Everyone knew the Craddock house, even if you were only passing through. The property had a plaque displayed out front declaring it a historical landmark. As one of the five founding families of Silverlake, a Craddock had lived at the estate for nearly two hundred years. Well, until Mr. Craddock passed away. As far as I knew, another family member had yet to take up residence. The Craddock house was located across from the lake, between the campground and business district. The house had been built up a bit, allowing for relaxing lake views and tranquility. When I was a little girl, Mr. Craddock used to host summer barbecues to celebrate the town's birthday. There'd be barbecue chicken, corn on the cob, potato salad, and so much pie. I remember stuffing myself silly, racing through the property's hills, and staring wide-eyed at the view.

When I pulled up to the house, I stared wide-eyed for a different reason. Someone had scattered all of the furniture about the front lawn. I parked my car at the back of the driveway and stepped out. A young woman who had been taping up a box in the garage stopped what she was doing and walked forward.

"There's not much left, but you're more than happy to look around. If it has a blue sticker, somebody's already bought it." The woman motioned to the yard.

"That's okay. I was hoping to talk with you, or at least I think you. Is your last name Craddock?" I took a chance. The young woman had shockingly bright blonde hair and blue eyes, much like Mr. Craddock had sported in his prime. It was hard even to notice a difference when his hair turned white.

"It is. I am Gabby Craddock."

"Nice to meet you, Gabby. My name's Angelica Nightingale."

"Are you related to Thelma Nightingale?" Gabby interrupted me.

Everyone knew my aunt. Even people who only visited Silverlake once or twice knew her.

"She's my aunt. We own the Mystic Inn around the bend." I pointed in the general direction even though you couldn't see the property from here. "I'm not sure if you heard, but we've had a little bit of drama in this little town of ours." I wasn't sure how else to describe the situation going on with Harvey and the break-ins. I didn't dare mention the mystery man's death. "A young man was cursed last night, turned to stone."

"Oh, that's awful." Gabby covered her mouth in shock.

"It is, but there's more to it. The young man was working here last week. I'm trying to find out if maybe you would recognize him and if something about him jumps out at you?" I took out my phone, brought up the photo app, and showed Gabby Harvey's picture.

Gabby folded her arms across her chest and leaned in to examine the picture. "Yeah, I remember him. He didn't talk much except to a friend of his. I didn't even catch their names."

"What about this?" I swiped to the next picture and held up the picture of the ring.

Gabby pursed her lips in concentration as she studied the picture. "Sorry, it doesn't look familiar.

But my grandmother had a lot of jewelry. You might want to check in with Katie down at Splendid Gems."

The mention of the jewelry store caused my ears to perk up. "The jewelry store?"

"Katie purchased the jewelry. Everything except for my grandmother's wedding ring. We did the same with almost everything else, selling it off in lots or donating it. My brother, John, took the books to the library and the clothes to the thrift store. I like the idea of my grandparents' things getting some use out of them as opposed to sitting in boxes in a storage unit. Alchemy Estates handled the rest of it." Gabby motioned to the front yard with her hand.

My mind started to whirl. I wondered if one of Harvey's coworkers had spotted something valuable at the estate, like a ring or necklace, and set Harvey up after it was sold to Katie. It was one theory that was worth taking a closer look at.

"Gab, are you coming up for lunch?" Gabby turned around toward the man standing on the front porch. His voice was clipped as if he was agitated. The man glared at me, but didn't bother to say hello, so I didn't either.

"Yeah, I told you I'd be right there." Gabby snapped back. "Sorry, my brother's had an attitude since we got here."

"I better let you get back to it then. Thanks

again, and if you think of anything, no matter how random it seems, give the inn a call."

"Don't worry, I will. Good luck."

I left the Craddock house and headed over to the jewelry store. It was a little early as most of the Village Square shops didn't open until later in the morning, but I was taking a chance that Katie might be in early. It turned out that Katie pulled into the parking lot right after.

"Just the woman I was looking for," I said as I got out of the car and shut the door after me.

"Me? Why, what's going on?"

"Did you hear about Harvey?"

Katie shook her head, looking pensive as she approached the shop's front door.

"He was turned to stone last night after Loretta posted bail."

"What?" Katie dropped her keys and bent down to retrieve them.

When she stood up, she'd already realized what that meant. "So, Harvey was telling the truth?"

"At least partially. He might have a partner who turned on him."

Katie looked over her shoulder. "Thanks for letting me know. I'll be sure to keep an eye out."

Katie unlocked the door and seemed surprised when I followed her in. She must've assumed I'd only stopped by to tell her about Harvey.

"Wow, this place looks amazing. How'd you get it cleaned up so fast?"

"It wasn't that bad. The hardest part was cataloging everything and figuring out what was missing. I was able to conjure the replacement glass from Witch-Mart. Thank goodness it's a standard size. Mike McCormick helped me install it."

"It looks great."

"Inventory's a bit low, but I know Deputy Jones recovered some of it."

"Speaking of inventory. I wanted to ask you about the jewelry you bought from the Craddock estate."

Katie looked taken back. "You think it's somehow connected?"

"It's an idea. I was at Loretta's house a little bit ago, and we found this ring in Harvey's pillowcase." I brought up my phone once more and swiped to show Katie the picture.

She squinted her eyes while assessing the image. "I don't know it. It's not one of mine."

"Harvey didn't steal it from here?"

"No, they found loose diamonds on him and a ring, but that's it as far as I know."

"Another ring? What does that one look like?"

Katie hesitated for a moment. I'm not sure why. But then she said, "It's a work in progress. I don't think the client wants me talking about it. It doesn't matter, though. The police still have it as evidence. But, if you want to talk about the Craddock estate, I can show you what I bought. It's a lot of costume jewelry, but I was willing to pay five hundred dollars for the box after seeing how well everything was preserved. It's mostly rhinestones and less precious gems, but still beautiful."

I followed Katie into her workroom. She led me to an oak jewelry box and lifted the lid, revealing a blue velvet interior. "These are the brooches up top." Katie slid open one of the drawers, "Then you have the bracelets." She slid open the third drawer, "And a couple of necklaces with matching clip-on earrings."

I craned my neck to get a better view. Katie was right; they were pretty, sparkling under the fluorescent lighting. The artificial lighting did nothing to diminish their beauty.

"And Harvey didn't mess with the box at all?"

"Nope, him and whoever he was with went for the good stuff. They knew what they were doing."

"Interesting. Okay." Maybe there wasn't a link to the Craddock estate, and Harvey had won the opal ring in a poker game like he had told his grandmother. It was unlikely, but not impossible.

"If you want to double-check on the ring, you can stop by Alchemy Estates. They inventoried everything. If Harvey stole it after they cataloged it—"

"Then they'll have a record of it," I finished Katie's sentence.

"Exactly."

"Hello, are you open?" Katie and I both looked over at Mr. Skyler. He held a loose gold watch in his hand. "I was hoping you could help repair this clasp. It snapped right off this morning."

"Sure, come on in." Katie waved the man forward.

"I'll catch up with you later, okay?" I said to Katie and then turned around to leave, waving goodbye to the history teacher on my way out the door.

Chapter 10

I had never stopped in Alchemy Estates before, but I was familiar with the strip plaza where it was located. The business was nestled between the grocery store and a coin laundromat. I parked in one of the spots in front of the building and scanned the business's hours to see if they were open. Thankfully, they were.

I pushed open the front door and took in the space. It looked like Alchemy Estates also sold various packing and shipping supplies. They had different sizes of packing tape, padded envelopes, and broken-down boxes available to purchase. A thick roll of brown packing paper that you could unroll and pay for by the foot hung from brackets on the wall. Photographs of family and friends, trips around the world, and furry animal friends made the retail space feel more personable. Like you were visiting a friend's house versus a business in a strip mall.

"I told you I would land the Hawthorne estate," the woman said to the man next to her with a twinkle in her eye.

"And did I say that you wouldn't?" he teased back.

"I believe you said something along the lines of, 'Are you sure you don't want me to go with you?'" She lovingly mocked him.

The man shook his head. "You're trouble. You know that?"

"But that's why you married me."

"Only one of your many fine qualities." The two shared a look. They must be newlyweds in addition to being new in town.

I smiled at the couple's playfulness.

"Don't mind my husband. We're not usually this rude." The woman eyed the man at her side, daring him to contradict her.

He cleared his throat. "Welcome to Alchemy Estates. How can we help you today?"

I walked closer to the counter and brought out my cell phone. "I was wondering if you could help me identify this ring? I'm trying to trace it. It might have come from the Craddock estate. I'm told you inventoried everything?"

"That we do. Let's have a look." The man held

out his hand to see a picture. I readily brought the image up and handed my phone over.

His wife peered over his shoulder. "You know what, that does look familiar. The Craddock's had a lot of beautiful pieces."

The man stared at the image. "I think you're right," he added.

"Hang on, let me go get the file." The woman slipped into a side office and came back moments later with a thick manila folder. She laid the file on the counter and opened it up, flipping page after page of spreadsheets. I attempted to read the file upside down. The first column held a picture of the image, followed by a description and then the price. The woman's index finger tracked down the page. She stopped on the fourth page. "I was right. Here it is. A two-and-a-half carat opal ring with baguette diamond accents. Is there something wrong with the piece?" The woman looked up expectantly.

"No, it was found at a friend's house, and we weren't sure how it ended up there." I was explaining the situation badly, but I didn't really know these people, and I wasn't sure how much I should actually say. "Do you have listed who the purchaser was?"

The woman trailed her finger further down the column to a blank space. "No, it doesn't look like it sold."

I clucked my tongue on the roof of my mouth.

So, Harvey must've stolen it. That was interesting. "How much is that ring worth?"

The woman consulted the paper once more.

"We appraised it at fifteen hundred." It was the husband that spoke this time, pulling out a separate sheet of paper.

"Who has the ring then? You said a family member found it?" the woman asked.

I sort of had to elaborate now. "We think one of the guys working for you last week stole it from the estate. That's the only thing that makes sense. Is the item insured?" I hoped Loretta wouldn't do anything drastic with the ring, but in case she threw it away or something along those lines, I wanted to make sure the Craddock family at least got the value of the ring returned to them.

"Of course. We're bonded and insured," the man replied.

"I don't know about the moving company, though." The woman looked back at her husband.

"Moving company?" I asked.

"We're a two-man crew, just Cecelia and me."

"We outsource everything else. Montgomery's Movers were the men on site clearing everything last week," the woman added.

I nodded. It looked like I'd be paying Mr. Montgomery a visit next.

"Do you think you can get the ring back?" the woman asked me.

"I'll sure try." I didn't want to add that the ring might be tossed or even in police custody. I wasn't sure about the details of the contract between Alchemy Estates and the Craddock family, but I knew someone would want it back.

I left Alchemy Estates after chatting a bit more with Cecelia. It turned out her husband's name was Jeffrey. Like me, they were transplants from Chicago, but they had traveled everywhere.

"Where was this picture taken?" I had asked seeing the rolling ocean behind the smiling couple.

"Spain." Cecilia gave her husband a knowing look.

"We spent our honeymoon diving off the coast," Jeffrey added.

My eyes had roamed the rest of the photographs. It looked like the couple had back-packed in Europe, explored the pyramids in Egypt, and climbed the Andes in Peru. Just looking at the photos had me aching for adventure.

"We should hang out sometime," Cecelia offered.

"Yeah, I'd like that. I'd love to hear more about your travels."

"Oh don't say that. You'll never get Jeffery to stop talking." Cecelia smiled at her husband.

"I'm not even offended because it's true," Jefferey quipped.

I was already picturing the four of us—Cecelia,

Jefferey, myself, and Vance hanging out from time to time. Living in a small town was nice, but sometimes I missed meeting new people and trying new things. It gave me something to look forward to, even if it was only going out to dinner with a new couple.

After I used my phone to look up where the mover's office was located, I put the car into drive and let my mind wander. Something about what Jeffery said to me stuck out. He said they appraised the ring for fifteen hundred, but Katie had only spent five hundred on the jewelry box. I wondered if that was right or if Katie should have paid more? Or, on the opposite, if Harvey and his buddies, maybe even Derek, stole more than one piece. It was something to ask Katie about. I was just a few minutes away from the moving company's office when I quickly called Deputy Jones and told him about the ring. I worried that if I called Loretta and told her Harvey had stolen it, she would get rid of the evidence. No, it was better to take her by surprise and send the deputy to fetch it.

"What is it this time, Ms. Nightingale?" Deputy Jones chuckled while saying the words. I'd long since learned to call his direct line when discussing a case.

"I found out Harvey stole a ring from the Craddock Estate. It's a two-and-a-half carat opal flanked with two baguette diamonds. Loretta and I found it this morning hidden in Harvey's pillowcase.

Alchemy Estates just confirmed it came from the Craddock house. I thought you should know."

"I appreciate that. I'll send someone over there to pick it up."

"Oh, also, Loretta doesn't know it's stolen. I just found that out."

"I see. I guess I'll head over there right now."

"Thank you." I sighed, waiting on the line, wondering if the deputy had any information he'd be willing to share with me.

"Yes?" The deputy drew the word out after a pause.

"I don't know. I told you something." I let the implication hang in the air.

"You know that's not how this works."

"I know. Just like I know I'm your best shot at solving this case." I bit my bottom lip. Maybe I'd pushed it too far, but trying to unravel this mystery and finish wedding preparations was making me testy.

"Are you sure you don't want me to transfer you over to the sheriff?"

"Hey now, that's just low."

The deputy barked out a laugh. "Alright. Alright. Listen, if I hear anything that's not confidential, I'll be sure to pass it along. Right now, we don't have a lot to go on. Harvey spent most of his time working odd jobs for Mr. Montgomery and hanging out with Derek and drinking beer on the back roads."

"And his cell phone?"

"Worthless. He had a prepaid plan and ran out of minutes months ago. The thing couldn't even connect to the internet."

"That's disappointing."

"Tell me about it."

"What about the mystery man?"

Deputy Jones sighed. "I'll say this. Until we have a cause of death, there's really no point in speculating."

"I suppose you're right." I still wasn't convinced and Deputy Jones could tell.

"If it makes you feel any better, I don't think they're connected. The man was staying at the bed and breakfast. Shannon said he'd told her he booked the place for a little R&R and to get some work done. His story checks out."

"What do you mean?"

"He was a professor working on a research article, taking advantage of summer break and our slower pace. If I were you, I'd focus on Harvey. Drop this mystery man business. I have a feeling the poor man's time was just up."

I thought about that statement and Deputy Jones was probably right. I needed to focus on the facts and not speculate. I told myself going forward, I would try and do that. "You make a good point.

And thanks for passing on the Harvey info," even if it wasn't much. It was true, Deputy Jones didn't owe me anything, but I liked to think we had sort of a working relationship. We both, after all, wanted the same thing for Silverlake, and just because I didn't have a badge didn't mean I didn't want justice. If anything, not having a badge allowed me to skirt around the rules. Look at me, becoming a witch vigilante. Who would've ever thought it?

I stopped by Montgomery Moving only to learn from the receptionist that Mr. Montgomery was on a job. He was at the music store, helping to clear the space out for a renovation. Of course, the music store was practically where I had started from, close by Alchemy Estates. At this rate, I was going to keep driving in circles around the lake all day, which was fitting because so far, that's all this case felt like I was doing, going around in circles. I pulled in front of the music store and saw Mr. Montgomery standing outside with his arms crossed over his chest. He watched as his men attempted to maneuver a piano through the shop's double doors. I knew the man by proxy. He was a lifelong resident, but I had never talked to him.

"You gotta move to your left, Carter!" The man bellowed. He moved forward to help, but his knee gave out, and he buckled forward. Catching himself, he said, "Your other left! Easy now. Easy!"

I knew it was a bad time to interrupt, so I stood

to the side, waiting for a free moment. It wasn't until the men had loaded the piano onto the trailer waiting nearby that I approached the gruff man.

"Excuse me, Mr. Montgomery?"

"Mr. Montgomery's my father," he grunted, limping forward to get closer to the workers.

Er, right. What was I supposed to follow up with to that? I pressed on anyway. "I'm sorry to bother you, but I just had a question about one of the guys that works for you, Harvey Johnson?"

"Haven't seen him." Mr. Montgomery, or whatever he wanted to be called, didn't take his eyes off of his men for a moment.

"No, I know where Harvey is at."

"Then what is it that you want?"

"I was wondering if you'd had any problems with him in the past?"

Mr. Montgomery's gaze flicked over to me. "What did you say your name was?"

I hadn't. "It's Angelica Nightingale."

"Thelma's niece."

"That's right."

"She back in town?"

"Huh?" Oh, we were still talking about my aunt. I was too busy watching his crew maneuver an upright base. I cringed as the top almost hit the frame.

"DUCK!" Mr. Montgomery said in the nick of time. The leader dropped his shoulders and thus, lowered the height of the instrument. The case grazed the doorframe. I winced. Mr. Montgomery growled in frustration and then turned to me. I realized he was still waiting for my answer.

"No, but she'll be back soon." She was coming home for Percy's wedding. "But back to Harvey, what can you tell me about him?"

Mr. Montgomery grunted. "Not the most reliable kid. Him and that buddy of his."

"You mean Derek? Is he here?" I looked around the parking lot but didn't see him. A stream of workers continued carrying instruments out, including a snare drum, a few cymbals, and black plastic cases that looked to hold tubas, given their shape and size.

"Nope, haven't seen either one of them, but then again, I'm not surprised. They're what you'd call unreliable."

I blinked at the man's response. That was practically a speech, given his previous replies. Mr. Montgomery surprised me by continuing. "They worked when they needed the money, and I can't be too picky. But what about you? What did Harvey do now?"

"I'm doing his grandma a favor. He got into a bit of trouble. I told her I'd help try to sort it out."

Mr. Montgomery frowned. "Loretta's always covering for that kid, calling in sick for him, making sure he has lunch money. It's like working with a ten-year-old half the time. If our families weren't close," Mr. Montgomery let his thoughts trail off as two men attempted to maneuver an expensive-looking harpsichord through the doorway. "Hold up, boys! Cole, Zach! Give them a hand!"

CRASH! The sound of metal cymbals clanging onto the cement snapped our attention. "Aw, come on, Kaden!" Mr. Montgomery grumbled something under his breath. I thought I heard the words *dang kids*, and *I'm getting too old* if my ears weren't mistaken.

"Listen, I'm really busy here. If I take my eyes off these kids for one second, something gets broken."

"No, I understand. Just one more question."

Mr. Montgomery's gaze flicked to mine. "Do you know who else Harvey hung around with besides Derek? Any of these guys?" I motioned to the other movers.

"Just Derek, as far as I knew. They pretty much kept to themselves."

"Perfect, thank you." As much as I didn't want to, it looked like my next stop was The Crossroads.

Chapter 11

"You want to go where?" Vance asked when I told him the game plan.

"I don't want to go there, but I think we need to. You know Derek knows something."

Vance weighed his options. I wasn't crazy enough to go out there by myself, but if he didn't go, I'd find someone else who would, like Clemmie, and he knew that.

"Okay, but next time you get a night off we get to do something relaxing, and not potentially suicidal," he relented.

"Excellent."

"Let me swing home and pick up my backup wand."

"Um, backup wand?"

"We might need it. I'll be there in thirty minutes."

I hung up with Vance and had a moment of hesitation, but I quickly dismissed it. The Crossroads wasn't that bad, was it? I was a kid last time I'd been out there. I was much older, smarter, and more powerful now. Surely nothing bad would happen.

Magic crackled in the air as soon as we crossed through the last four-way stop that signaled the beginning of The Crossroads. I could feel my power hum in my veins in response to the shift in the atmosphere. Out of the corner of my eye, I saw something black run through the corn field. It disappeared in an instant. If I'd blinked, I would've missed it. I had no idea if what I saw was a shifter or an animal, and I wasn't sure I wanted to know. It made me think the community had spies, shifters keeping track of who entered their territory.

"Strong, powerful witch," I muttered to myself. It was my mantra whenever I needed a confidence boost. Only I hadn't realized I said it out loud.

"What was that?" Vance said from the driver's seat, turning to glance at me.

"Just a pep talk," I replied with a winning smile.

Vance reached over and squeezed my hand.

We turned down the grass and dirt road. Nothing out here was paved. The county hadn't even cut in the roads. It was as if the outcasts had set up an outpost and a neighborhood built up around it.

The houses ranged from doublewides with detached garages to sheds with tarps for a roof and corrugated metal sides. I even spotted a pop-up camper. Kids ran barefoot through the front yards playing tag. A litter of puppies chased them, or those might have been shifter kids. It was impossible to know. A woman hung up her washing on the line. She followed us with her eyes when we drove by. Two older men did the same. They were sitting on their front porch. One wasn't wearing a shirt. I didn't even bother to wave.

"Right there." I pointed to the neon orange trailer. It looked like Dereck had spray painted it hunter safety orange. The paint was uneven, making the baby blue undercoat peek out in places.

I didn't have high expectations for the inside.

I was wrong.

Derek's trailer wasn't like Harvey's bedroom.

I peered in through the front window. It wasn't hard to do since he didn't have blinds or curtains. The living room was spotless. The furniture was mismatched, yard sale finds most likely, but the carpet had been recently vacuumed. I could still see the lines in the carpet. Derek also didn't have any dishes or dirty socks thrown around.

Vance knocked. "Hey, Derek. You home?"

I looked to Vance and raised my eyebrows.

There still wasn't a response a couple minutes later.

Vance tried again, knocking louder. "Derek? I need to talk to you about Harvey."

Vance shrugged. I knew what the expression meant. He figured it wouldn't hurt to drop Harvey's name since Derek already wasn't opening the door. Maybe he'd change his mind if he knew why we were there.

But there was still no answer.

Derek didn't have a garage, but he did have a chain-link fence surrounding his trailer. Honeysuckle had grown over the fence. The metal bowed under the pressure of the wood weaving through it.

"I don't see a car. I wouldn't mind checking out the backyard though."

Vance looked from side to side. "It might not hurt to have a better look inside. Derek might be turned to stone, too."

"I hadn't even thought about that. How about I do it?" Vance started to protest. I held up my tiger's eye necklace.

"You're going in as a cat."

"Easier that way, don't you think?" That way Vance didn't have to try to lift me up to look into the windows. I could walk along the window ledge.

Normally, I never do a transformation spell right out in the open, but this was The Crossroads. I doubted no one would think twice witnessing my shift. If anything, they might quit staring at us. I swear eyes were everywhere.

I gripped the tiger's eye stone around my neck, closed my eyes, and said the incantation that would transform me into my feline alter ego: "Metamorfóno alithís ousía." The necklace channeled the magic and released it in a burst. Bright, white light surrounded me. Heat flooded my body as atoms rearranged themselves and altered my reality. In an instant, the spell was complete.

Vance easily picked me up and set me on the window ledge. I scampered along, disappearing into the backyard. I stopped and looked into the first window. It was the kitchen. Derek had dishes drying on the rack. There wasn't so much as a wayward spoon left in the sink. There was also no sign of Derek.

The next window was Derek's bedroom. The bed was made, and his dirty clothes were thrown into the bin by the door.

I started walking again, careful to balance on the edge, when I heard something. It was a continuous, rhythmic clinking sound. It took me a minute to place it. It wasn't until I walked to the back of the trailer and felt heat coming out of the dryer vent that I knew what it was. It was a sound of coins rolling around in the dryer drum. If the dryer was running, Derek was definitely in town. The washer was going too. I could hear it now that I was listening for it.

Unfortunately, I needed to get back to the inn.

There was still so much to do. Tomorrow morning was Eleanor and Percy's bridal shower. Clemmie was hosting it. I needed to make sure we had all the raffle prizes ready to go.

I jumped off the window ledge and pranced on my paws back to the fence. My head was already back at the inn, thinking about everything I had to do when a dog ran at me out of nowhere.

"WOOF! WOOF!" The booming barks came from behind me.

I gave an impressive "ROWW" and hightailed it out of there. Vance scaled the fence in two seconds. The chocolate lab and I were running full tilt. I jumped up into his arms. Unfortunately, I transformed in the process and hit his chest with a WHUMP.

Vance stumbled backward, my weight adding to the momentum, and we went down, hard. We both rolled over onto our backs, trying to catch our breaths.

Thankfully, the pup was a good boy. He sat on his haunches, his head cocked, looking at us and wondering what had happened.

"I'm so sorry. Cat instincts. I panicked," I said in between breaths.

Vance tried to inhale. "Wind ... knocked ... out."

I grimaced, and stood, offering Vance a hand up. He took it, and we stood.

"Hey, buddy, what's your name?" I leaned down and reached for the dog's collar.

He lowered his head, unsure if he should trust me or not.

"Sorry, didn't mean to scare you." I could only imagine what the dog thought seeing me transform from a cat to a person. And I was almost positive he was a dog and not a shifter. You couldn't fake that hesitancy. Not to mention the name tag. Most shifters tended not to wear collars. Although, this was The Crossroads; anything could go.

I reached out and petted the dog's head and checked out his name tag in the process. "Hi, Gunner. Where's your owner at, huh? Is he home?"

Gunner's tail wagged back and forth in the patchy grass.

"You sure he's a dog?"

I fingered the name tag around the animal's neck. "Pretty sure."

Vance looked down at the worn metal tag in between my fingers.

"I'd say so."

"Derek has to be around here." I motioned to the doghouse and the fresh water. "And the dryer is going."

"Where though?"

"I don't know, a neighbor's house? Or maybe he isn't home at all, but he will be soon."

Too bad I didn't have the time to sit around and

wait. If only there was a way to know when Derek would come home. I thought for a moment, my head cycling through every spell I knew. Then it came to me. "I've got an idea. Follow me."

I gave the dog one more pat, told him he was a good boy, and then made my way to the front door. "I read about this spell in the Modern Witch's Guide to Exes and Hexes. It's a text charm. It keeps track of who comes to your door." Ideally, it would alert you if your ex, or anybody for that matter, showed up on your doorstep. In this case, I was going to set it so that I would get a text notification when Derek came home.

"That's a brilliant idea," Vance replied with a look of admiration.

"I have them from time to time."

I traced my wand over Derek's doorframe. A soft green light emitted from the tip as I warded off the place. It's not that I didn't want anyone to go in, it was that I wanted to be alerted when they did.

"You're a bit scary, do you know that?" Vance joked.

"Thank you, I try." The truth was I spent so much time learning how to curse people to protect myself that I should switch and start working on healing spells. I thought back to when I was a child and how many times Aunt Thelma had to whip out her wand to sooth a scrape or take the burn away from a bee sting. It was time for me to do the same.

My wand continued to glow a faint green color as I said the words, "As above so below, when someone crosses, I will know." I repeated the phrase, my eyes transfixed on the door. When the rectangle was complete, the entire door lit up a brilliant green before fading. "Now when Derek comes home, we'll know to come back to question him." The only downfall was, who knew when that would be, and would he still be home when we made it back?

Vance and I stepped off the porch and were walking back to the truck when I saw someone unexpected.

"Mr. Skyler?"

The history teacher faltered. He was walking down the driveway opposite of us. "It's Angelica, right?" He tried to recover, but I could tell he looked uncomfortable.

"Right. This is my boyfriend, Vance."

"Nice to meet you."

"We were just checking in on a friend," I explained, hoping he would add what he was doing out here. Mr. Skyler was a clean-cut, khaki-wearing type of guy. He wasn't Crossroads material. Unless it was all an act?

"Tutoring," Mr. Skyler stuttered. "I'm out here tutoring. A couple of the boys want to take the state GED exam. I'm helping to make sure they pass."

"That's great," Vance remarked.

"I'm sure they appreciate that," I added.

"Not everyone," Mr. Skyler said with a fake smile plastered on his face. "I've got to get going. Good seeing you."

We parted ways in the middle of the street and headed on our way, his car followed Vance's truck out of the makeshift community.

Chapter 12

The following morning, I headed to Clemmie's tea shop, Sit for a Spell, for the bridal shower. I'm not sure what it was. Maybe visiting The Crossroads had me paranoid, but I felt like someone was watching me as I walked through Village Square, but every time I turned behind me, no one was there. The feeling caused the hair on the back of my neck to rise. It didn't help that I was walking through the shopping center alone in the early morning hours. I wanted to get to Clemmie's early enough to put out the finishing touches like the white paper liners filled with candied almonds and a bridal word search for guests to fill in to pass the time until everyone arrived. Plus, there was the food. Even though Eleanor couldn't eat, some of her guests could. We expected a mixture of both the living and unliving at today's soiree. When Eleanor decided on a morning shower, Clemmie worked with Diane to provide a variety of scones, muffins, fresh fruit, and jams. Diane said she'd throw in some bite-sized desserts as well, because what's a tea party without sweets?

I had never been so happy to walk into Sit for a Spell. Thankfully, the moment I arrived, I was swept up into setting up for the shower and I forgot all about the morning stalker vibes.

Clemmie's shop was set up with one side servicing as a retails space and the other as in-house dining. Customers could take their purchases and snack on them next door or even arrange for formal tea service. Each of the shop's round tables could seat six guests. Clemmie planned to drape the white tablecloths with a swath of lavender to match the wedding colors over the tables before the guests arrived. In addition to being on the town council, Diane's husband, Roger, was also a florist. He arranged glass globes full of white roses as center-pieces. The arrangements offered an understated elegant look.

Like the bridal shower, the wedding was set to take place in the morning only at the church. The couple chose to host a breakfast following the service, a tradition in Eleanor's time. I thought a wedding brunch was a lovely idea.

At first, I wasn't sure what to get a couple who seemed to have everything. Eleanor was planning on moving in with Percy at the inn following the wedding, not a day before, and we had everything they'd need. But then I remembered how much Eleanor loved to read. When she was cursed to the tavern, she told me she had spent many days and nights reading tales of love and adventure until she could go on one again. With that thought, I picked up a volume of poetry from Spell Binding Books. It was a new-to-me poet, mostly love poems. Something that I hoped she hadn't read before. Although Eleanor could surprise you. The ghost recently told me she had bought an e-reader. Still, I knew she'd appreciate the golden gilded pages and ribbon bookmark the poetry volume came with.

Much later, after visiting with all the guests, eating several strawberry tarts, and drinking copious amounts of tea, I finally had a chance to give Eleanor her present.

"Well, isn't this just the most precious gift?" Eleanor looked at me with tears in her eyes. "I love books." She turned the volume over and read the back of it. "Love poems, how fitting." She looked at Percy and winked. Percy hadn't been paying attention. He was looking longingly at the remaining strawberry tarts, but not to throw them. Something about his expression look pained, as if he was longing to pick up the dessert and eat it once more. That last thought gave me an idea. Although, it was an idea that I would have to check in with Connie about. Connie was a potion master and owned the local potion shop. If a spell was possible, Connie would find a way.

I realized Eleanor had said something else, but I hadn't caught it, being off daydreaming.

"What was that?" I asked her to repeat it.

"I was saying I hope no one comes in and steals this book."

"Someone stole one of your books?"

"Well, technically, they didn't seal any of them, but they sure did make a mess."

"To your books?" I wanted to make sure I was following Eleanor correctly. It couldn't be a coincidence that someone had broken into Misty's bookstore and ransacked Eleanor's bookshelf.

"It was most particular. I mean, my books are all antiques—favorites even. I'm not sure what anyone else would want with them. But when I came home from dinner with Percy last night, I found half of my books on the floor."

"I told her I didn't know anything about it," Bonnie chimed in. Eleanor lived above the tavern Bonnie and her husband, Daniel, owned, since Eleanor was Bonnie's great, great aunt.

"You don't by chance have cameras, do you?" I asked Bonnie.

"We don't, but I think we need them with everything that's been going on lately."

I agreed as much as I hated to.

Bonnie's comment seemed to get the rest of the guests talking about Harvey and the recent break-ins.

"Are you taking the case?" Vicki, Misty's manager, asked me. At the same time, Clemmie questioned, "How close are you to solving it?"

I hated to admit that I was no closer to solving the case today than I was yesterday or the day before. "But information like someone messing with your books is helpful. Make sure you report that to the sheriff, or better yet, call Deputy Jones." I had a feeling all these seemingly insignificant clues were stepping-stones to the truth.

With all the interest in books, I thought it would be best to head to the library and see if anything was amiss. As far as I knew, no one had attempted to break in and ransack the place.

Mrs. White was working the front counter. She was a sweet old lady who simply refused to retire. "I love my job too much!" she said with a smile when anybody ever brought up retirement.

Silverlake's public library was down the street from the school. It was a single-level, tan brick building with a circular drive and side parking lot. I had loved visiting the library ever since I was a small child. Since I'd been back in town, I'd spent more time admiring the books at Misty's bookstore than making the drive around the lake to the library. Still, something about walking through the library's double doors reminded me that the library was magical too. I'd have to make a conscious effort to stop in more often. It probably wouldn't hurt to read more, too. It might help me relax and not feel so stressed out. I rubbed the knot forming at the top of my right shoulder blade as I cut across the library's floor and headed to the women's fiction section. I bypassed the mysteries, figuring I had enough of my own to solve. I skipped the horror section as well. I was a scaredy-cat when it came to violence. Maybe I would pick up a romantic comedy instead. Something lighthearted and fun. A little bit of escapism. Wasn't that why I loved reading so much? Books gave me a chance to jump into someone else's life for a little while. I plucked the first two covers that spoke to me off the shelf and carried them to the circulation desk.

"Angelica? It's been an age. So good to see you." Mrs. White took the books from my outstretched hand.

"Hang on. I have my card in here somewhere." I began digging around my wallet, wondering where my card went. I found my old insurance card, debit card, and even my loyalty reward card for La Luna, but no library card. "I'm afraid I can't find it. I must've left it in my old wallet when I switched them out." Which meant it was safely in the bottom of my dresser drawer.

"That's okay. We can get you set up with a new

one." Mrs. White skipped asking me for my identification and proof of residency. Everyone knew where I lived. I began filling out the application, putting each letter and number in the corresponding rectangular space on the form.

"Here you go," I rotated the form and slid it back across the desk a few minutes later.

"And here you go," Mrs. White handed me a new card across the desk. While I was filling out the application, she had entered my personal information off the top of her head. The older woman then scanned the application and compared it to what she had on the screen. "I just need to put in the updated phone number," she remarked. I waited a moment while her keyboard clicked, and she inputted my digits. After that, Mrs. White checked out my books and slid those across the counter as well. "Enjoy the books. They're due back in three weeks."

"Thanks so much. Listen, before I go, I was wondering if anything suspicious has happened here lately? Someone tried breaking into Spellbinding Books, and I just came from Eleanor's bridal shower, and she told me someone ransacked her bookshelf. Given the focus around books, I thought I'd check with you."

"Interesting you should ask. I reinforced the wards after the high school break-in, and just last night, they went off."

"They did?"

"Mmm-hmm. My firecracker charm woke up the whole neighborhood. It made enough noise to raise the dead."

"What time was that?"

"Oh, I guess it was around eleven o'clock. Mrs. Meyer across the street called me. She said the bang gave her a heart attack. I was awfully sorry about that, but I was glad the spell worked."

"A firecracker charm. That's a good idea. Do you have a copy of the spell?"

"Let me make one for you. It's in the library's reference section, Encyclopedia of Spells, Volume Three. I'll only be a moment."

I reread the back cover of one of the books I had checked out and then turned to start chapter one while waiting for Mrs. White to return.

I hadn't even read a paragraph before Deputy Jones greeted me from behind. "You following up on the book lead?"

"I am, actually. Did you know the wards went off here last night?"

"I do now. You sure you don't want to join the department?"

"Not unless you're sheriff," I said with a smile. Deputy Jones and I were both kidding. As much as I liked solving mysteries, I loved managing Mystic Inn even more.

"What's that?" I noticed the deputy had a slip of

paper sealed in a clear plastic bag. The card had a series of numbers written in columns across it. They almost looked like dates given the dashes separating the numbers.

"I'm not sure. I'm hoping Mrs. White can help me with it."

"Mind if I take a look?" The deputy hesitated. "You never know, I might be able to figure it out."

"But be careful." The deputy relented. I accepted the bag and took a closer look. I was right, the numbers did look like a date, but sometimes the first and second numbers went higher than a calendar did. For example, the first column had the digits 6–17–75. That could very well be June 17, 1975. But the second set of numbers was 25–99–2. Sometimes there were even three digits. I wrinkled my nose, trying to figure out what else the numbers could represent. "What about combinations for a safe?"

"That would be a lot of safes."

"True. I am trying to think of what else takes three sets of numbers."

"I know. I typed a few strings in an Internet search, but that didn't help me either. I tried several different ways."

Mrs. White took up her post behind the counter and handed me a copy of the spell. "Here you go," she said with a smile, and then she looked down at the paper Deputy Jones and I were studying.

"Oh! A cipher. I haven't seen one of these in ages. Are you here for the book?"

"What book?" The deputy and I said in unison.

"The book that goes with this code."

"Wait, what is this?" I asked.

"It's a book cipher. Look here. The first number is the page of the book. The second number is the line on that page. Then the third number is the word."

"And these all go with the same book?" Deputy Jones asked.

"They should. Do you know what book you need?" Mrs. White directed the question to Deputy Jones.

"I have no idea. Would there be a clue anywhere on this that might help me figure that out?"

"Not if it's a good cipher." Mrs. White shook her head. "You wouldn't want the source material listed anywhere. It would defeat the purpose."

That made sense. "So, people send secret messages back and forth using these numbers?" I wanted to make sure that I understood.

"That's right. People have used ciphers to swap messages for hundreds of years. They're time-consuming to write, but efficient as long as you know what book was used."

"And we don't." Deputy Jones huffed.

I understood his frustration.

How many books were there in the world? A

hundred million? More? I wasn't sure how we'd know to pick the right one.

"I'm sorry I can't be more help," Mrs. White started to say.

"You already helped plenty. I didn't even know what this was when I walked in here. I'm glad I thought to stop in. You're always a big help." I had to agree. Librarians were smart and resourceful. I'd have to keep that in mind.

Mrs. White walked away to reshelve a cart of books and left the deputy and me alone. "Not that you have to tell me, but where did you find that?"

Deputy Jones scanned the area to make sure nobody was eavesdropping. "It was in Harvey's back pocket when we brought him in for questioning."

My eyes lit up. "Oh, what if it's a message telling him to be at the jewelry store at a given time?" I rapidly snapped my fingers with excitement. "That would prove Harvey went to the jewelry store will-ingly. There might even be information here telling us he knew they would rob the store!" My magic grew tingly at the prospect.

"It very well could. The only problem is, we need to find the book."

"And we're not the only ones looking for it."

"How do you know that?"

I tried to explain my jumbled thoughts. "Think about it. Someone attempted to break into the library. They did break into Spellbinding Books, and they also ransacked Eleanor's bookshelf. They're obviously looking for a specific book." I bit my bottom lip, trying to think this through. "Here's my working theory. Tell me what you think. Harvey could have the book or at least know what book it is, and he's using code to communicate with his accomplice. Someone else knows about the code and what Harvey is up to, and they're trying to get their hands on the book to either beat Harvey at his own game or maybe blackmail him?"

"It's not a bad theory, except for one point. Do you really see Harvey going through all that trouble writing ciphers and cracking codes?"

"Er, no." Sadly, I did not. "Maybe Harvey's the one who's trying to track down the book? Wait, no. Mrs. White said someone tried to break into the library last night after Harvey was already turned into stone. I don't know. I'm at a loss here." I scrunched up my nose.

"I'll keep thinking on it."

"I know you will. I'll do the same. Question, when you were at Harvey's house, did you see any books sitting around?"

"I didn't see any books, but he did have magazines." I didn't look closely at them, but I remembered seeing them stacked on his bedside table.

"I suppose it doesn't have to be a book."

"No, I'd imagine any written source material would work."

"Maybe I'll stop back over there and see if I can make any of this make sense."

"Were you able to recover the opal ring?"

"I did. Loretta was surprised I knew about it." The deputy raised his eyebrows at me knowingly.

"I knew she wasn't going to call it in." I wondered what else Loretta would be willing to hide from the authorities. She said she wanted to uncover the truth, but what if the truth was that Harvey was as guilty as we all assumed? Then what would she do? I had a sinking feeling that we might find out.

"I'll head back over and see about the magazines. If you talk to her, you might want to keep the book cipher out of the conversation."

"I'm already one step ahead of you. I don't know how much we can trust her."

"I agree. Loretta might destroy evidence and then ask for forgiveness later."

I then had another question. "You know the break-in at the high school? Any idea what the thief was after?"

"I'm not sure it's related, but it was Mr. Skyler's room."

"The history teacher?"

"That's him. The person broke into the outside door to his classroom."

"I wonder what for?"

The deputy shrugged. "Mr. Skyler's going

through his things, but so far it doesn't look like anything is missing."

"Huh." Mr. Skyler was the teacher we ran into at The Crossroads. I wondered if there was any connection.

"Deputy Jones?" Mrs. White called out.

The deputy snapped his head up and strolled over to meet the librarian, leaving the cipher on the counter.

"These are all the code books we have. Not sure if it's any help," Mrs. White said, leading the deputy down an aisle.

I didn't waste any time, taking out my phone and snapping a picture. I tucked my phone back in my purse just as quickly and went back to nonchalantly looking at my books.

Deputy Jones and Mrs. White returned a few minutes later. I pointed to the cipher. "I didn't want to leave this unattended," I said with a straight face. It wasn't a complete lie.

"Thanks for that." Deputy Jones slapped his hand on the bag and slid it off the counter.

Chapter 13

I was getting ready to follow the deputy out the door when my friend Luke walked in with his twin nieces, Sabrina and Beatrice. It had been a minute since I'd caught up with the candy maker, so the two of us stood and chatted in the entryway while his nieces took off for the teen section.

"How have you been? Business good?" I asked. Not so long ago, all of Silverlake's businesses were suffering, but luckily tourism had steadily turned around. It was something that I, along with the other business owners and the town council, was constantly trying to improve.

"It's been steady but not amazing."

"Yeah, I can agree with that." I was fortunate that I didn't have to compete with much business in town besides the bed-and-breakfast and the campground. But even I wasn't sold out most nights. I was hoping things would pick up more rolling into summer here.

"I wanted to talk to you and see what you thought about promoting a Good Old Days of Summer week, or something like that? I know we have the town bicentennial coming up, but that's not until fall. Do you think it's too late to pull something together for summer?"

I hated the thought of adding something else to my plate at the moment, but Luke had a point. We could be doing more to promote our town. I had hoped Mayor Parrish would step up and take over advertising, but she seemed content leaving it to us. I will say this was a better alternative to how she used to be actively protesting our efforts.

"Let me think on it a bit. Maybe not a full week of events, but we could probably do something over a weekend." I pictured a raft-building contest complete with a race across the lake. Maybe a volleyball tournament or a sandcastle building contest, too. The shops in Village Square could host sidewalk sales, and we could ask the town council to spring for complimentary popsicles or lemonade. The ideas began to swirl in my head. I reached for my purse to pull out my cell phone and jot down notes.

"Sabrina, noooooooo!" Beatrice wailed. Luke's head popped up. An alarmed expression crossed his face. Who knew what trouble those two were into?

Laughter, the library could deal with. Mischief was something entirely different.

"I better go," Luke said as he stepped in their direction.

"It was nice seeing you!" I continued to rummage in my purse, which was more like a tote bag today. I thought it was smart with everything I wanted to take to the bridal shower to have a larger purse. My plan paid off as I pushed the two hard-cover books to the side and dug to the bottom for my cell phone. I pulled my wand out and went to tuck it under my arm to get it out of my way when Mrs. White's voice startled me from behind.

"Wonderful! You're still here!" I jumped and gave a little squeak. Unfortunately, with my fingertips on my wand, the energy transferred into a spell. A purple puff of smoke hissed out of the end of my wand. It smelled suspiciously like rotten eggs sitting in a hot car on a summer day. My eyes immediately began to water as I fanned the air in front of my face. "I'm so sorry! You startled me." Mrs. White coughed into her fist and backed away, fanning the air in front of her. I thought she was going to retreat, but the next moment she withdrew her wand and muttered a wind spell. I ran forward and pushed the library's front door open to blow the stink out.

"That'll teach me to sneak up on you again," Mrs. White teased.

My cheeks flushed with embarrassment.

"Again, I'm so sorry. What is it you wanted to say to me?" I quickly changed the topic. It was either that or perish on the spot.

"Oh yes, that's right. You asked me if I had noticed anything strange lately. It wasn't until I overheard Deputy Jones mention Harvey that I remembered he was here a few days ago."

"Really? Did he check anything out?"

"Well, that's the thing. He tried to steal a book. It was quite strange. He could've easily checked it out. It wasn't a reference copy. But he tucked it in the front of his pants of all places. I was standing right by the door when he walked out, and the sensor went off."

"What did he say?"

"He gave me some baloney about wanting to read it in his car. He didn't think he was doing anything wrong. After I told him the book had to stay inside, or he could check it out, he begrudgingly opened an account."

"What book was it?" Could this be the source material we were looking for?

"It was a book on the town history. Vivian Merryweather wrote it."

Misty's middle name was Merryweather. I wondered if Vivian was related to her? "You don't by chance have another copy of it, do you?"

"I'm afraid not. But let me write down the title for you."

"Thank you. I'd appreciate that."

Another minute later, I had the book title in my hand and was finally walking out to my car. No one jumped out at me, but I did have an eerie feeling wash over me. I kept up my pace, but my eyes scanned the parking lot. My hand instinctively reached in my purse for my wand. I put my wand in one hand and my car keys in the other.

I clicked open the lock on the car doors and opened the driver's side door at the same time Gabby's brother, John, drove slowly past me. His foot wasn't even on the gas, he just idled past, watching me.

I stared right back, wondering what the heck his problem was. When our eyes locked, he turned abruptly and gassed it out of the parking lot.

I stared after his car for a moment. "What was that all about?"

Chapter 14

I didn't want to get Deputy Jones's hopes up in case the book turned out to be nothing, but I had a good feeling about it. I drove on autopilot to Village Square, and beelined it for Spellbinding Books. Vicki was ringing up a customer when I came bustling through the door.

"Angela? Is everything okay?"

I could only imagine what my face looked like. I schooled my features. "Yeah, I'm looking for a book. I'm really hoping you have it."

"Is it the new Hex Time thriller?" Clemmie asked. "Because if so, I'm afraid I bought the last one. But I'll lend it to you when I'm through."

"No, although I do want to read that. But what I'm looking for is a Silverlake history book written by Veronica Merryweather."

"Oh, I know that one. That was written ages

ago," Vicki remarked. "It should be over here in our local section. If it is about Silverlake or written by one of our residents, we'll find it over here."

Clemmie and I followed behind Vicki, weaving through the aisles until we came to a stop in front of a small section. The space was only two sections wide and three shelves tall. "It's alphabetical," Vicki explained, trailing her finger down the spines. Her finger passed from Marvin to Newton. No matter how much we looked, we didn't see any book written by Miss Merryweather.

"Huh," Vicki put her hand on her hip. "I swore I just saw it, unless we sold it, but I filed inventory last night. Let me check the computer."

We marched back up to the register. Vicki began to type on her keyboard. Her confusion etched deeper on her forehead. "That's what I thought. It's showing we have one in stock."

"Unless someone stole it. I was just at the library and Mrs. White said Harvey tried to walk out with it earlier in the week."

"Come again?" Clemmie questioned. I went on to explain the book cipher and how this history book might be the source material. "Is there a way to conjure another copy?" If it was in stock somewhere, Vicki could order a new copy and conjure it instantly from someplace like Witch-Mart. Of course, you could always conjure something from a stranger, but that was stealing.

Vicki clicked on a couple more screens. "I don't think so. It looks like it's out of print."

I twisted my lips while thinking. "You know what it looks like though, right?" I asked.

"Sure, I can picture it in my mind. You want me to try to use a summoning charm?"

"That's what I'm thinking. Maybe it's here somewhere and it was filed on the wrong shelf."

"That's not a bad idea. I used to volunteer at the circulating desk over at the library. You'd be amazed how many people put books back in the wrong spots."

"Let me grab my wand." Vicki disappeared to the back office where employees kept their personal belongings and came back with her wand momentarily.

We spread ourselves around the bookshop. Vicki stood in front of the register. Clemmie covered the upstairs by standing on the top step to survey the space, and I hung out in front of the local shelf where the book should be, in case we somehow managed to overlook it. Clemmie and I gave Vicki space to clear her thoughts and picture the book. When she was ready, Vicki raised her wand and said, Éla edó."

I stared at the shelves before me, but nothing glowed.

"I see something!" Clemmie shouted, causing a nice young man to jump. "Sorry about that," she replied to the man sitting off to the side. He was probably enjoying being lost in a good book until Clemmie startled him. "Up here," she turned her voice back down to us.

You would think we were after buried treasure with the way we hustled up the stairs. There, sitting right front and center at one of the study tables was the book. I was shocked to see it there out in the open. I thought for sure it had been stolen, or if it was here, it would be hidden somewhere. But no, the book was glowing faintly just waiting for us to find it.

Clemmie beat me to it.

Downstairs the shop's door opened, and Vicki looked disappointed to see another customer walking in.

"Be with you in a moment," she hollered down to her.

"Do you have the cipher?" Clemmie asked as I sat down at the table and pulled the book toward me.

"I do. I snapped a pic with my phone. Here, let's see what we find." I went to the first three-digit string and carefully went to page six then to the correct line and word number seventy-five, counting out loud. The first word was community.

"Community, got that?" I looked over to Vicki and Clemmie.

But our success was short-lived because there

wasn't even twenty-three lines of text on the next page as the cipher indicated.

"You sure you're looking up the right page?" Clemmie leaned over my phone and looked at the code and then back to the book.

"I'm positive and look, there aren't even three hundred pages in this book and the last word is on page three hundred seventy-five."

"Then what did Harvey want with this book?" Vicki asked.

"Good question. I'm going to buy it and figure it out." I doubted Harvey was into history so much that he was willing to steal a book from the library for some light reading. There had to be a clue here.

I took the book and walked next door to the diner. Vance's mom, Heather, owned the restaurant, and it was one of my favorite places to grab a quick bite. I couldn't help it, I loved Heather's monte cristo sandwich and her sweet peach iced tea. Heather swung by my table as soon as I sat down for a quick kiss on the cheek. She flipped over a glass and filled it with iced tea without me even asking.

"My son meeting you?"

"I hope so. I'm going to give him a call right now."

"Tell him I made rhubarb pie," Heather said with a wink.

"Will do."

"How did the shower go?" Vance asked after we said hello.

"Good, I think Eleanor had a really nice time.

I've been busy since with this case, though. Do you want to meet me for a late lunch at the diner?"

"Sure, I'll be there shortly."

"Do you want me to put in an order?" I didn't have a ton of time with the wedding rehearsal still today.

"Sure, tell my mom to surprise me."

"She made rhubarb pie."

"I'll see you in two minutes."

It turned out that Vance walked in the door before I even had a chance to flag down the waitress. "You really did only mean two minutes."

"I was next-door catching up with Brody."

"Oh, what's new with him?"

"Hmm?" Vance's eyes wandered around the diner, probably looking for his mom.

"What's new with Brody? Anything?"

"Ah, not much. He's planning a fishing trip out of Vero Beach. He was wondering if I was interested."

"That sounds like a good time. When's he thinking of going?"

"What's that?"

"When's Brody thinking of going on the trip?" I followed Vance's gaze wondering why he was so distracted.

"Oh, um ... you know, he wasn't sure yet. Probably sometime in the fall. Hang on, I'll be right back." Vance excused himself from the table and greeted his mom with a hug. The two disappeared into the kitchen, and I shook my head. Vance obviously had something on his mind, and hopefully his mom would help clear it.

I decided to take a look at the history book while waiting for him to return. I flipped through the book and scanned the pages. The binding wasn't very thick, only about an inch. The book had a hard glossy front cover with a picture of Wishing Well Park on it. The prose was written very much in textbook fashion. It felt like reading a history book, because it was a history book. The pages were full of old photographs, like the original pictures of village square and the business district when all that was there was the community church and courthouse. I was still looking at the book when Vance strolled back to the table, a broad grin on his face.

His expression caused me to smile in return even though I felt like I was missing something. "Everything okay?"

"Yes, absolutely. Sorry for walking off, where were we?"

We had put our conversation on hold once more to place our order. It was only then when our waitress walked away that I was able to fill Vance in on what he had missed this afternoon.

"So, Harvey had the cipher on him, and he tried to steal a book," he summarized.

"This book." I tapped my fingertip on the cover. "I'm not sure why. The cipher doesn't match it."

"He might have not known that when he tried to walk out with the book though," Vance pointed out.

I weighed Vance's remark. "That's true, I didn't think about that. Okay, maybe there's nothing important in this book." That would be disappointing.

"It doesn't matter if it's a good idea or not!" A man shouted from the other side of the diner.

Vance and I snapped our heads over toward the commotion.

My eyes scanned the table, quickly recognizing the town council members. It was Terry Myers who'd raised his voice.

"I wonder what they're arguing about?" Vance said to me.

"We want this to be the best bicentennial celebration there's ever been," Mayor Parrish's voice rose above the grumbles.

I looked to Vance. "Well, now we know. Speaking of the bicentennial celebration, Luke asked if I'd be willing to brainstorm some summer promos. I told him I would see what I could come up with."

"Do you have time?"

"No." I replied flatly. "But Luke brought up a good point. If we don't market Silverlake, tourism will dry up again. I don't want that to happen, and I know you don't either."

"No, but I don't want you getting run down, either. Why don't you draft up some ideas and see if Luke wants to chair it?" That wasn't a bad idea, but knowing me, I'd have a hard time handing the reins over. Vance saw the hesitation in my eyes. "Or at least co-chair it," he grinned.

"You do know me well."

"Don't you think we should at least try?" Sam Hamish, another council member, suggested.

"I don't think there's any harm in that," Mayor Parrish chimed in.

Vance and I attempted to ignore the council members squabble while we ate our lunch. The diner was busy, which was normal for a Saturday afternoon. "I don't know how much business you need to drum up, things look steady here," Vance remarked.

"That's because your mom makes amazing pies." Tourists could forgo Luke's Candy Cauldron, but you'd be hard-pressed to find guests who didn't want a slice of Heather's famous pecan pie.

"I'm not going to disagree with you there."

"Oh look, that's Jeffrey and Cecilia Harcourt. They own Alchemy Estates; I wanted to introduce you to them." I waved at the couple, and they approached our table. "Hey, how are you guys doing?"

"This place is fantastic," Jeffrey remarked while taking in the diner's retro decor.

"Vance, this is Jeffrey and Cecilia. Vance's mom owns the diner," I said to complete the introduction.

"Look at that pie case." Cecelia nudged Jeffrey's arm with her elbow. "How are we ever going to choose?"

"Guess we'll have to just keep coming back."

"Any recommendations?" Cecelia asked me.

"You can never go wrong with the pecan pie. The nuts come right from Wishing Well Park."

"Really? That's amazing." Jeffrey then moved in closer and lowered his voice. "Not that I want to talk about work..." Cecilia gave her husband a dirty look. He smiled sheepishly. "I promised Cecilia I wouldn't, but that was before we ran into you."

"Oh, fine. I suppose I'll forgive you, but just this once." Cecilia shook her head in mock disbelief.

"I wanted to know if you ever found that ring. The one from the Craddock Estate?"

"Oh, yeah. Deputy Jones retrieved it. It might be evidence right now, I'm not sure. But I'll make sure he gets in contact with you."

"Perfect, thank you." Jeffrey then turned to his wife. "I'm done. I swear I won't bring up work anymore today." Cecelia raised her eyebrows as if she didn't believe that for a minute.

"It was nice seeing you," she said at the same time Vance replied, "Nice to meet you."

"They seem fun," Vance remarked after they walked away.

"I thought so. Might be nice to hang out with them sometime. They're from Chicago."

"I don't know. I might never get a word in."

"Stop. We'd be sure to include you every half an hour or so," I teased.

Vance went to the register to pay, and I told him I would meet him outside. I was waiting for him when Mr. McCormick stepped outside. He looked at me and shook his head. "Maybe you should be on the town council."

I shook my head. "No way. I heard you guys in there. What's all the drama about?"

"No one can agree on anything. I wish Thomas was still alive. People respected the man."

"Mr. Craddock had been on the council for a long time, hadn't he?"

"Over forty years. There was something about him. He had a way of settling disputes. The council needs someone like that."

"What's going on? Is there anything I can do to help?" Not that I needed anything else on my plate, but I couldn't resist the call for help.

"No, it's foolish really. Terry wants to display the Silverlake Sapphire, but it's a moot point, none of us even know where it is."

"The Silverlake Sapphire?"

"You know, the magical sapphire that protects

Silverlake from the outside world?" I knew mortals couldn't see Silverlake, but I never thought about the magic that went into the illusion. In order to enter Silverlake, you had to cross an old rickety bridge that appeared to go to nowhere. Anyone with a lick of common sense would turn their car around. The bridge didn't look like it could hold a bicycle let alone an automobile.

"I've honestly never heard of it, but it makes sense. You guys lost it?"

Mike shook his head. "It's not lost, it's protected. It's all in that book of yours right there." Mr. McCormick pointed to the history book tucked under my arm. "The founding fathers took it upon themselves to protect the stone. Not one person knows where the stone is kept. They each only have a piece of the puzzle."

My mind raced at warp speed to try to make sense of where Harvey might fit into this. "What about Mr. Craddock's piece of the puzzle? What happened to it?"

"That's the thing, none of us know. It wasn't where it was supposed to be." I noticed Mr. McCormick was purposely being vague, but I had a feeling I knew what Mr. Craddock's piece of the puzzle was.

"And his grandkids don't know anything about it."

Mr. McCormick shook his head. "Not a clue.

They weren't very close with their grandparents. There's a divorce somewhere in there," he said as if that explained everything, and in a way, it did.

"Can I take a guess? It was a book cipher, wasn't it?"

Mr. McCormick looked shocked. "How do you know that?"

"Because I believe Harvey Johnson and whoever he was working with is trying to find the Silverlake Sapphire." I went on to briefly explain how Harvey helped clean out the Craddock estate last week and was found with the cipher. "He also checked out this book," I motioned to the history book tucked under my arm. It turned out the book wasn't useless, not if it included information about the sapphire. "I think the person behind the break-ins are trying to find the source material."

"You mean the code book."

"Do you know who has it?"

"Not a clue. There's not a single council member who knows all the secrets, not even Mayor Parrish. It's by design to keep the sapphire safe."

"And it's worked for the last two hundred years," I remarked.

"Which is why I think we should just leave it alone. Wherever the sapphire is, it's power is still working. Putting it on display is asking for trouble."

"Normally, I'd agree with you, but somebody's

already hunting for the stone. It might be a good idea if the council tries to beat them to it."

Mr. McCormick sighed in frustration. "Why do people have to cause so much trouble? Why can't they just leave well enough alone?"

"That is an excellent question. I wish I had the answers for you."

"Well, it was nice chatting with you, Angelica. I'll keep what you said in mind."

"Good luck." I watched the council member walk away and wondered if there was a way they could find the stone and protect it, or even re-hide it.

"What's wrong?" Vance said when he stepped outside the diner and read my expression.

"What do you know about the Silverlake Sapphire?"

Vance and I fell in step with one another. "Isn't that an urban legend?"

"No, I guess it's very much real. Why haven't I ever heard of it?"

"You mean to tell me Aunt Thelma never told you the legend as a bedtime story?"

"No, she always read from Gwendolyn's Magical Tales before bed." I loved those stories. I remember my aunt would perch on the side of my bed with the leather-bound book and let me pick out the evening's adventure. There were one hundred tales in that book, but I stuck with the same handful of stories about witches who slayed dragons and defeated the evil fairy Prince.

"Another fine example of classical literature for the young witch."

"It is, isn't it? They were the best." My mind flashed forward to the future, and I envisioned reading my own children the same magical tales that had mesmerized me as a kid. I tripped over my feet at the thought of having a family. Vance caught me as a pitched forward.

"Are you okay?" We stopped walking. Vance looked at me, waiting for me to respond, but I stood there dumbfounded looking up at the man that I knew was my future.

I cleared my throat and started walking again. "Sorry, I just tripped going down Memory Lane." I tried to make light of my stumble, but inside, my heart was hammering in my chest. My head tried to catch up with my heart. Of course, I knew that when Vance and I rekindled our relationship a family might be in our future, but I just hadn't expected to feel so strongly about it so soon. Maybe it was my age, or maybe it was the fact that I loved Vance unconditionally, and I knew he felt the same way. He loved me for who I was, Type A personality and all. There's something comforting about a person who knows your faults and still chooses you every single day. I couldn't dwell on lovey-dovey feelings though. I tucked my feelings away and focused on the matter at hand. "Remember how the town council was just arguing? Mr. McCormick told me it's about the Silverlake Sapphire. Some of the members want to display it for the bicentennial celebration, but they don't even know where it is. The founding fathers each hold a clue to the location, or something like that. I guess there's more information about it in this book." I motioned to the book under my arm.

"And the Craddock family is a founding family."

Vance already knew where this was going.

"Mr. Craddock was responsible for the cipher."

Vance nodded in understanding. "Harvey stole the cipher from the Craddock house."

"What I can't figure out is how did he know to look for it? Someone had to have sent him in to get it, and I bet it's the same person who broke in and turned him to stone."

"And the same person who's going around breaking into places looking for the book."

"So, who is that person?" I tried to think back to my conversation with Loretta and what I knew about Harvey.

"You said Harvey worked for Montgomery Movers?" Vance asked.

"Yeah, I paid Mr. Montgomery a visit to see what he could tell me about Harvey. He said that he wasn't really a reliable employee, but he couldn't afford to be picky."

"Do you think he could be behind it?"

I pictured the gruff older man in my head. He was definitely stressed out trying to keep an eye on everyone. Plus, a lifetime of physical labor wasn't easy. I wasn't sure what had happened to him. He really couldn't move around as well anymore with that pronounced limp of his. "You know, he could be. His job is stressful, and his physical strength isn't what it needs to be for that kind of work."

"If he knew about the cipher, he could use it to steal the sapphire, make a quick fortune, and retire," Vance replied.

He might be on to something. "I think we need to look into his background and see what his financial situation is. I know he said Loretta was a long-time family friend, that's why he had hired Harvey. So, there is a connection there other than Harvey working for him."

"I wonder if there was any sort of relationship between Mr. Montgomery and Mr. Craddock? Think about it, that house is huge. Harvey must've had some indication where the cipher was in order to be able to find it."

"You bring up a good point, like maybe Mr. Craddock was friends with Mr. Montgomery and he told him about it?"

"I can't see Mr. Craddock revealing the cipher's location, but maybe Mr. Montgomery was a friend and had been in and out of the house searching for it over the years."

I then got a sinking feeling in my stomach. "Vance, do you know how Mr. Craddock died?" All I knew was that it had been sudden, but I hadn't given the cause of death much thought until now.

"Do you think he was murdered?"

"I think we need to find out the cause of death to make sure that he wasn't. Let's say Mr. Montgomery is our bad guy and he knows about the cipher. What if he killed Mr. Craddock to get him out of the way?" I was already taking out my cell phone and dialing Deputy Jones's line before Vance could reply.

"Tell me you solved this case," Deputy Jones said when he answered the phone.

"How did Mr. Craddock die?" I replied, catching him off guard.

"Come again?"

"I'm working on a theory, and it might involve Mr. Craddock's death."

"You're going to have to back up. Walk me through this."

I went ahead and filled Deputy Jones in on the past couple of hours and our current working theory.

When I was finished. Deputy Jones was silent on the other end.

I waited another moment before breaking the silence.

"Deputy Jones? Did Mr. Craddick die of natural causes?"

"No." The word hung in the air. "I'm looking at his autopsy report right now. We thought it might have been a slip and fall. Mr. Craddock had been found dead at the bottom of his stairs while still in his pajamas."

"That's awful. I hadn't heard."

"No one has. The family kept it quiet. This information doesn't go beyond you and Vance, do you understand?"

I looked up at Vance. "We understand," I said speaking for the both of us.

Vance cocked his head realizing that the information must be important. I would've put my phone on speaker, but we were standing outside Village Square where anyone could overhear.

"Mr. Craddock died of a broken neck and not from the fall. Dr. Humphrey said the bones were twisted."

"Twisted?" The word whispered past my lips. My stomach dropped realizing that meant someone broke Mr. Craddock's neck.

"You better be careful, Angelica. This isn't some New Year's Eve prank or a wayward curse. We have a violent criminal on our hands."

"No, I understand. We will be," I said when I

was able to find my voice. ""Do you have any suspects?"

"Not yet. Not even a person of interest, and I swear if that leaks to the press, I'll never tell you anything about a case again."

"My lips are sealed. In the meantime, you might want to look at Mr. Montgomery. Harvey was working for him, and they both had access to the house. With Mr. Montgomery's health not being so great, that might give him motive."

"Good thinking, I'll take it from here. If Mr. Montgomery is the killer, he's dangerous. You best stay away."

Deputy Jones didn't have to tell me twice.

Chapter 16

I hung up with the deputy and took Vance's hand, pulling him over to the side away from any bystanders.

"Things just got much more serious." I then told Vance how Mr. Craddock had died and that there'd been a change in plans. Deputy Jones was going to spearhead looking into Mr. Montgomery.

I looked down at my phone. I still hadn't gotten a text alert that the door charm at Derek's had been tripped. Could he really not have come home yet? I then thought of the chocolate lab, Gunner, that had given me a heart attack. If no one had crossed the threshold, then no one had come to take care of him.

Vance realized what I was doing. "No alert yet?"

"Not yet." I frowned. "We need to go back." Part of me really hoped that the charm hadn't worked, and Derek had come home to care for his dog, and if he was home, Vance and I could give them a heads up. I remembered that Harvey was with Derek when he was arrested. I'd be shocked if Derek didn't know who Harvey was working for. Heck, Derek was probably working for him too. I wasn't even sure if Derek knew that Harvey had been turned into stone, but somebody should tell him. Maybe Vance and I could scare him straight and get him to give up the name.

"Gunner," Vance remarked.

I nodded. "It's possible that my spell didn't work, but I was sure I set it. You saw the door light up, didn't you?"

"I did."

"As much as I want to drive out there right now, I have the wedding rehearsal first." I wanted to skip it, but as the official wedding planner, I couldn't not show. "You mind coming to the church with me? The rehearsal should probably only take a half hour."

"That's fine, we can do that. Then you want to head back up to The Crossroads?"

"I think that would be a good plan." Eleanor and Percy wouldn't have even needed a rehearsal if the wedding party didn't include so many little ones. Eleanor had asked her great, great, great (yes, three generations back) nieces to act as flower girls. Percy's great, great-grandsons were acting as ring bearers.

All together, there were six young ones set to walk up the aisle. Additional family members were going to do the scripture readings, and even Bonnie and her husband Craig were set to perform. I hadn't known the two were so talented until I heard them one night before closing singing karaoke at the tavern. The duo could give any act in Nashville a run for their money. All this to say, there were plenty of people that had to know where to be and when, hence the rehearsal. I only hoped it wouldn't take too long. We had a mystery to get to the bottom of.

VANCE and I stood outside the church and looked up at the gargoyles perched on the ledge, three stories high. The only thing taller was the church's bell tower, which chimed on the half-hour and hour. Plus, it tolled a little tune at noon. I'd gotten so used to the sound that I barely noticed it anymore. The chimes blended together with the birds and small town chatter, creating a soundtrack that was uniquely Silverlake.

"He was a good boy," Vance remarked, remembering the time the gargoyles had come to life and Vance had adopted one of them for a bit. After guarding the church for close to two hundred years, the beasts needed some downtime. The vacation was short-lived, however, and after a few weeks,

Rocky had resumed his post on top of the church. His partner had done the same, and now both gargoyles were back where they belonged.

"What is your problem? You are acting like a child!" Vance and I looked across the street to where Gabby was arguing with her brother on the courthouse steps.

"It's wrong and you know it. You're just too stupid to do anything about it," John shot back.

"Stupid? Really? Now I know you're a child. When are you going to grow up?" Gabby looked weary.

John kicked the ground and stalked off. Gabby turned and walked back to the car.

"Okay, then. Shall we go inside?" I said to Vance because I was not about to stick my nose in a family dispute. I had enough drama to deal with.

Soon after, Vance and I hung out at the back of the church and watched everything unfold. I gave Percy a nod of encouragement as he stood at the front, waiting for Eleanor to float up the aisle and meet him. In addition to singing, Bonnie's husband, Craig, was also walking Eleanor down the aisle. Everything felt like a regular wedding rehearsal except the bride and groom were ghosts.

It wasn't long before the wedding party practiced the processional, and they were currently going over the order of the ceremony.

"I don't know, maybe we could've skipped this,"

I whispered to Vance. Father George had everything well under control. You could tell he'd done this a time or two.

The priest covered the ceremony highlights, giving a condensed version of the vows Percy and Eleanor were going to say, omitting the "as long as we both shall live," phrase.

The couple practiced standing at the altar, facing one another. Eleanor blushed. They were an adorable couple. Just don't tell Percy I said that.

"Excellent, and then I'll say what God has joined let no man put asunder. Then the two of you will kiss, and we'll begin the recessional."

Percy leaned in and stole a kiss. Eleanor playfully swatted him on his shoulder.

As I watched the two of them together, I made a wish that they'd have many years of happiness.

Chapter 17

It was early evening as Vance and I turned on to the country roads leading us back to The Crossroads. Neither one of us said much; I used it as some down-time to clear my thoughts. The wedding was exactly one week away. The rehearsal ran smoothly, but I still had things to get done. I hadn't finished the programs or tied the ribbon around the book-mark favors Eleanor had picked out. Each wedding guest would leave with a care package that included some of the couple's favorite things. A bookmark, bubble bath, peppermints (Percy said he could almost taste them) and a whoopee cushion. Percy loved his practical jokes. I drew the line at the fake dog poo. I sighed. I'd switch back over to wedding planning mode after stopping by Derek's. I hung my arm out of the window and rested my head back on the seat, closing my eyes and being still for a moment.

Thirty minutes later, my head jostled to the side and woke me up with a start. Vance had slowed and was turning into The Crossroads.

"Sorry," I yawned and sat straight up.

Vance glanced over at me. "You don't have to apologize. I might have you drive on the way back, and I'll take a nap," Vance smiled.

"Are you kidding me? I want to take a nap on the way back, too."

Bits of gravel crunched under the tires as we continued into the community. I immediately noticed something was off. You didn't need magic to pick up on it. Everything was dead silent. There wasn't a person in sight, which was even more odd given that it was a beautiful June evening. I couldn't even hear a bird sing or a dog bark. Forget kids laughing. No one was outside.

"This is creepy," Vance remarked.

"It is." It reminded me of driving through a bad neighborhood and knowing everyone's eyes were on you, making you want to lock the doors and speed up, but The Crossroads was our destination. We weren't going to turn around now.

Vance pulled up to the house, same as before, and we hopped out of the truck. I waited on my side for him to come around and join me. Vance gripped me by the hand and tugged me forward. Both of us had our wands out in our other hand.

I swallowed uncomfortably. The hair on the back of my neck stood on end, and I felt like I was being watched by a predator, and I'm sure I was.

Gunner barked from the back gate. He pranced on his paws and wagged his tail. His nose stuck out through the fence.

"Hi, boy. We see you." I waved and gave a reassuring smile.

Gunner howled in response.

I frowned. Something about the sound didn't seem normal. Gunner backed up and turned his snout, almost as if he was motioning us to follow him.

"Hang on," I told him as Vance jogged up the front porch and rapped on the door. At first it was silent, followed by a bellowing bark. Gunner was not dropping it. Vance cupped his hands around his face and peered into the window.

"I don't see anyone."

"Let's go around and check the back. Gunner's trying to get our attention. Unless he just wants some pets. That's understandable if he's been all alone all day."

Vance and I stepped off the porch and walked around to the side of the house.

Vance saw the body before I did. He stopped

and tugged my arm back. "Don't look. It's bad." Vance took a step forward.

I'm convinced that was the worst thing you could tell somebody. Of course I was going to crane my neck to look.

I wish I hadn't. I really wish I hadn't. Derek was there, lying dead in the side yard. His neck was twisted at a gruesome angle, and something had been eating him. There was no other way to describe it. I was speechless. I opened my mouth to say something, but all I did was swallow back the queasiness that threatened to overtake me. "Keep your wand out," I hissed. We had our backs to one another so we could see any threat before it approached. But just like when we pulled into the subdivision, everything was deadly silent.

"What do we do?" I knew we had to call it in, but I didn't want to stand there like two targets waiting for whoever the killer was to strike again.

"Let's go back to the truck and drive out of here. We'll get a mile up the road and call it in."

I nodded. That sounded like a solid plan to me.

"And we're taking Gunner."

Vance didn't argue. I sidestepped the body and kept my eyes forward. The moment I opened the gate up, Gunner ran forward and jumped up on me, licking my face.

"It's okay, boy. We'll make sure you're safe." Gunner pranced around me. I hooked his collar with my finger and lead him over to the truck, making a wide arc around the body. I didn't want him to see his former owner that way. The pup easily followed.

Vance opened the back door, and Gunner jumped in. I sat in front and reached back to pet him. Gunner panted in response.

We wasted no time getting out of there and calling Deputy Jones. It would take them a bit to get out to us, but what else could we do? The Crossroads generally took care of their own mess. They weren't in Silverlake's jurisdiction, but given the tie to the Craddock case, they were making it their jurisdiction.

"What do you think ate him?" I said after he called it in. We were a bit outside of the community on the side of the road.

"I think maybe one of his neighbors," Vance said grimly.

"A shifter?"

"I wouldn't be surprised. Shifter or not, they are still apex predators."

I felt sick at the thought of it. "Did you see that his neck was snapped?" I looked back at Gunner. I don't know why. Maybe I was worried he could pick up on the conversation. He panted, looking out the window.

"Yeah, I saw that."

"I think whoever killed Mr. Craddock also killed

Derek and then one of his neighbors had a snack." I couldn't believe what I was saying.

"It would make sense. That many predators in one community probably couldn't resist."

"Oh, gross."

Sheriff Reynolds arrived with Deputy Jones a bit later. Twilight was fast approaching, and I didn't want to be out here when it was full dark. I shuddered thinking about it.

"YOU SAID IT'S PRETTY GRUESOME?" Sheriff Reynolds said as he strolled up to the truck. Vance and I got out to talk to the Sheriff and Deputy Jones on the side of the road.

"You're probably going to want a memory charm to bleach the images from your brain," Vance remarked.

The deputy and sheriff shared a look. I wished Vance had been joking. They had no idea what they were in store for.

"What made you think to pay Derek a visit?" The sheriff's questioning continued.

"Just trying to get a feel for what he knows," I answered honestly. "I promised Loretta I'd look into Harvey's case. If anyone knows what Harvey was up to, it would be Derek."

"Bet you're rethinking that plan now, huh?"

Sheriff Reynolds lowered his aviator sunglasses and looked at me over the top of them.

"No, not really." I could've gone without seeing Derek's body, but somebody had to find him, and we'd been able to rescue Gunner.

"Is there anything that jumped out at you at the scene?" Deputy Jones asked. "Anything we should know about?"

Vance and I shared a look. He spoke up first, "Everything was really quiet. I've been to The Crossroads before, and usually there's dogs barking and people staring at you from their porches. You know what it's like. There was none of that tonight."

"But I still felt like they were watching us." I turned as I said the last part to Vance to gauge his thought.

"Agree."

"Honestly, we didn't stick around. Once we saw Derek's body and realized people were watching us, we got out of there and called you right away," I added.

"What's up with the dog?" Sheriff Reynolds asked when Gunner popped his head out the window and barked.

"He's Derek's. I couldn't leave him there," I explained.

I waited for the sheriff to reply with some smart-mouthed comment, but instead he nodded. Who knew he was an animal lover underneath all that grumpiness? "I guess we better get going, before the body completely disappears," the sheriff said motioning for Deputy Jones to follow him.

I then turned to Vance. "What do you say, you ready to get out of here?"

"I've never been more ready in all my life." I had to agree with Vance. Aunt Thelma said The Crossroads was trouble, and boy was she right. If I ever came back out here again, it would be too soon.

Chapter 18

I woke up in the middle of the night to what sounded like someone in the room next door, but there shouldn't be anyone in Aunt Thelma's bedroom. I lay in bed listening again to see if I had truly heard something. The problem with living in a hotel was people were free to come and go as they pleased, and when you had guests staying on the floor below you, it made it hard to tell where noises were coming from. I'd adjusted to the noise over the past year, but tonight it was different. It sounded like someone had bumped into the adjoining wall.

I slipped out of bed and fumbled around in the darkness on my bedside table for my wand. My fingertips rolled the smooth wood my way, and I grasped it firmly in my palm. I then cracked my bedroom door open to see if I could see anyone. My plan was to hit the intruder with a stunning spell and then call Deputy Jones. It sounded like a smart plan to my sleep-addled brain, but in retrospect, it could've used some tweaking. Because when I opened my bedroom door, a pair of lime green eyes shone back at me from the living room. It was the same black cat that I had chased away from the hotel at the end of last week.

"Hey, little fella, how did you get in here?" I kept my voice light as if I was coaxing the kitty to come to me, when in reality I was thinking this could be a person and I had to keep my wits about me. I lived on the third floor. There was no way this cat got into my apartment unless a person was involved. I didn't have a ledge to scale or a window box to climb on. Certain town council members, like Mr. McCormick could appear out of thin air. But I didn't know of any who could blink into existence and transform into a cat. Magicking your way into existence wasn't a spell any old witch was allowed to cast, even if they were skilled enough. Legislation kept a tight rein on who could disappear and reappear in a snap.

I was also thinking that whoever this cat was, they were the same person who broke into the bookstore and quite possibly killed Mr. Craddock and Derek.

If this was a person, I bet they broke in when I was asleep and transformed into a cat after they knew they were caught. They were probably hoping

I'd only see them as a cat, and let them out the door. But little did they know, they weren't the only one who could transform.

That didn't mean I couldn't play along. "Are you lost little kitty? Maybe I should call animal control?" I held up my phone in one hand. My thumb was on my keyboard as I was typing a message out to Vance, telling him to come quick. The only thing that kept me from hitting the cat with the spell right that second was that I was not one hundred percent certain that it was in fact a person. It was the one percent that kept me from raising my wand. I couldn't bring myself to use a spell on a cat unprovoked. It seemed to break a witch code of ethics not to mention my heart. I loved animals too much.

I continued to text Vance, keeping an eye on the cat. He seemed to be doing the same, staring at me, trying to capture my attention. It worked. I kept looking up at the cat, wondering what he was thinking and making sure he wasn't ready to pounce. I was getting ready to hit send when I was suddenly struck with a spell from behind. I never saw it coming. The cat proved to be the perfect distraction. Well played, villain. I felt as if I had been hit with tunnel vision. Like I was folded in half and being pulled backward through a straw. Every-thing started to go dark around the edges. I first lost my ability to see. Next, I couldn't hear anything.

Lastly, my consciousness slipped away and I was left with nothing at all.

THE NEXT MORNING, I was lucky enough to wake up alive. My face was pressed into the living room floor. I could feel the indentation of the carpet fibers in my cheek. I pushed up off the floor onto my hands and knees and then sat back until my bottom was resting on my heels. My muscles felt stiff as if they had been locked all night long. I wiped my hand across my face and tried to take stock of everything. The apartment looked the same as ever. Looking down at myself, I too looked the same. In the daylight, I could see the bottom of my cell phone sticking out from under the couch. I crawled forward and slipped it free. Swiping up, I saw my half typed out message to Vance. I'd never had a chance to hit send. I didn't care what time it was, my finger found Vance's number, and I selected it to complete the call.

"Good morning, beautiful," Vance said while yawning.

"Vance, I." The words choked in my throat. I didn't know how to tell him what had happened. Somehow it made the events of last night all the more real.

Vance was immediately on alert. "What's

wrong?" I could hear what sounded like car keys followed by the shutting of a door.

Despite my best efforts, I couldn't keep from sobbing into the phone. "I was attacked last night. I'm okay," I quickly added. "Just sad, and mad, and I don't know what else." I wiped my cheek with the back of my wrist.

"I'm on my way. Did you already call Deputy Jones?"

"No. Can you come here first? I just really need you." I didn't want to answer a bunch of the deputy's questions and have to analyze what happened. All I wanted was for Vance to come over, and wrap me right up in a big hug, and tell me everything was going to be okay.

"I knew I shouldn't have left you last night." Vance had offered to stay the night or let me keep Gunner, but I'd insisted I was fine and the dog would do better at his place. Vance's ground floor townhouse had a private fenced off backyard and Vance still had everything from when Rocky stayed with him. I had told Vance I was going to take one of Connie's calming tonic's and go to bed, which was exactly what I did.

"Listen, I slept fine."

"Until someone broke into your apartment and attacked you," Vance snapped. I knew he wasn't mad at me, but the words still stung, and he knew that. "I didn't mean that. I'm sorry. I had a feeling."

Vance's voice trailed off. "Listen, I'm ten minutes away. I'll stay on the phone and let you know when I'm there so you can open the door." I could hear the truck engine roar.

I don't think it even took Vance ten minutes to get to me. Vance gave me a play-by-play as he drove halfway around the lake and pulled into the parking lot. "Percy's working the front desk. Now I'm coming down the hallway. I'll be right up," Vance continued to dictate.

Vance's knuckle barely grazed the door, and I tugged it open and fell into his arms. He crushed me to his chest and held me tightly with one arm while he closed the door behind us and wrapped both arms around me and kissed my temple.

We stood like that for a moment. Vance gave me the strength I needed to face my reality. I could have been killed last night. For the life of me, I couldn't figure out why I wasn't.

"That's it. Until this guy is caught, I don't want you alone at night."

"Vance—"

"I'm serious. If the roles were reversed and someone was after me, would you let me stay home alone at night? I can't let anything happen to you. You're my world, and I'm already sick with what could have happened. Please."

"Vance, I'm sorry. I didn't mean for any of this to happen."

"It's not your fault. I'm not mad at you. I'm mad at myself for not keeping you safe. I know you're brave and you're strong, but sometimes I want to be the one to take care of you."

A tear slipped down my cheek, and it wasn't because I was scared but because I was overcome by Vance's words.

"I like when you take care of me. When I let you," I added with a smile.

"Good, because I love you more than anything in this world."

"I love you too." Vance held me to his chest, and I was content to stay there the rest of the morning. Or I was until my brain started firing again. "Why did they break in, though? If they're looking for a book, they won't find it here. Aunt Thelma owns a handful, but she tends to leave them about the inn for guests to borrow."

"What do you mean they?"

"Remember the cat I saw the night you came home? It was here in the apartment. I heard a noise and when I went to investigate, the cat was sitting right there." I pointed to the back of the couch. "I figured it was probably a person. How else would they have gotten in?" I bit my bottom lip to keep from crying. Tears weren't going to solve anything, least of all this case. "But the cat turned out to be a distraction. I was hit with a spell from behind when I went to text you."

"The cat's not a cat."

I shook my head. "Not with a coordinated attack like that."

"Honestly? I think they did it to scare you. A way to tell you to back off."

"Well, if that was a goal, I can say it was a success." I was scared out of my wits. But I wasn't about to back off. No way.

Chapter 19

"Knock, knock!" Aunt Thelma's voice rang out as she walked through the front door. "Hello! Angelica, are you here?" Vance and I stepped apart. My eyes were still teary when my aunt surprised us.

"What are you doing here?" It wasn't the nicest welcome home response, but I was shocked to see her.

My aunt immediately scowled at Vance "What's wrong? What did you do?" I could only imagine what Aunt Thelma thought given our relationship history, and she had been out of town for the last six months. If there was anyone who was more protective of me than Vance, it would be her, and she loved Vance.

"Vance didn't do anything. He's comforting me." I sniffled, remembering his sweet words.

"Oh, well if that's the case, don't let me stop

you. I'll put my bags in my room."

Aunt Thelma went to do just that when I stopped her. "Actually, there is something I need to talk to you about. I was going to call you."

"I knew something was wrong. My witchy instincts were twitching."

"How about you put your bags away and I'll make us some tea."

"Now I know it's a disaster. It's nine in the morning, and you're making me tea. The bags can wait." Aunt Thelma dropped them right then and there inside of the door to prove a point. "Now come here, dear, and tell me what's going on."

It took a little bit to recap the past week. A display of emotions played out across my aunt's face ranging from shock to anger, to disbelief as we told our tale.

"You should've told me. I could've come home sooner."

"Honestly, I thought we had it under control until last night." I looked over at Vance to back me up.

He did. "Angelica's been brilliant piecing it together."

"No, it's not that." Aunt Thelma disappeared down the hall. Vance and I shared a look.

"What is she doing?" I whispered.

Vance shrugged. "You never know."

Wasn't that the truth. With Aunt Thelma, I've

learned to expect the unexpected.

She returned a moment later, a deep frown creasing her face. "It's gone."

"What's gone?" I asked.

My aunt suddenly looked weary. "The book."

"*The* book? As in the code book?"

"I'm afraid so. I was the keeper."

I couldn't believe it. "What? Why didn't you tell me?"

Aunt Thelma held up her finger. "First of all, you came home not that long ago. I had to make sure you were staying. Second of all, I'm nowhere near close to dying." Aunt Thelma shrugged. "I thought I had more time. And before you can say anything else, if I were to drop dead tomorrow, Terry Mandel knows I'm the keeper. He'd be sure to pass the information on to you."

At the mention of Terry's name, something clicked together. I remembered him raising his voice at the diner, wanting to find the gem. Could he be the one looking for it?

"Why Terry?" Vance asked.

"Each keeper has a second. Mike McCormick was Thomas Craddock's. Terry Mandel is mine. And no, I didn't know Mike was Thomas's until after Thomas passed."

"Why all the secrecy? Why not display the gem in a museum or keep it locked up in a safe, and be done with it?" I asked.

"How do you know it isn't?" Aunt Thelma countered.

"If people knew where it was, they wouldn't be killing one another and breaking into homes." I looked down at the table as I spoke the words.

No one said anything for a moment until Vance spoke up. "What book was it anyway?"

"Gwendolyn's Magical Tales." Aunt Thelma winked.

"You've got to be kidding me. That's the source material? I love that book."

"You do?" Aunt Thelma looked taken back.

"Why is that a surprise to you? You read to me from it every night when I was little."

"I just thought you liked books in general." Aunt Thelma did have a point. I did enjoy reading. "So, you see, I didn't keep the book from you. I just didn't tell you how magical it was."

"All this time, the book was right here. I can't believe it." I stared at the wall.

"And I would've told you all about it if you would've called," my aunt reminded me.

"Sorry, I thought I could figure this out on my own," I confessed. Not to mention I didn't want to intrude. Aunt Thelma could use a dose of happily ever after.

"And I have no doubt you eventually would have, but we can do it faster together." Aunt Thelma patted my hand. I hadn't wanted to drag her into this, but I had to be honest, it felt good to have her home.

Vance spent the next half hour cooking breakfast. He made blueberry pancakes, bacon, and strong coffee. It was comfort food, and I needed it. We had to come up with a plan to get the book back and catch the thief, or rather make it thieves, and possibly murderers.

I was finally starting to feel a bit more human after eating breakfast. Maybe I'd be able to think clearly with a full belly.

Aunt Thelma had her spell book open, looking for a way to retrieve the book. "We can try to conjure it. I know it's out of stock, but maybe you can nab a copy from someone else." And by nab, Aunt Thelma meant steal. When you conjured something, you were basically stealing it from someone else unless you pre-paid for it, like from Witch-Mart. Witch-Mart offered a pay now and conjure it program. It was why conjuring cash and jewels was illegal. It always came from somewhere. Oftentimes, criminals would get sloppy with their spell work and authorities were able to trace them.

"If only I knew who had a copy of it, I'd borrow one," I remarked. It was too bad that it was out of print.

"Hang on, if you love the book, then why don't you use a tracing charm?" Vance asked. He had started on the dishes. A sponge was in one hand, cleaning the frying pan, and he had a dish towel slung over his shoulder.

I blinked at my boyfriend. Not because I didn't know what a tracing charm was, but because the answer was so obvious. Tracing spells combined magic and emotions. You had to love the object or person you were tracking down in order for them to work. Vance knew all about them from helping me on a previous case.

"Do you truly love the book?" Aunt Thelma asked.

I thought back to my childhood. The nights all blurred together, but the book was always there. I smiled thinking about it. "I do."

"Then let's see what you can do." Aunt Thelma winked and pushed my plate forward.

I closed my eyes and took a deep breath in through my nose and out my mouth. I tried to relax and enable my magic to flow freely through me. *Don't hold back*, I thought.

In my head, I pictured the book's cracked spine and burgundy leather cover. I bit my bottom lip to concentrate and bring the image into focus. The memories broke free and floated forward.

Suddenly, I could see the scrolled lettering, spelling out the title and the picture of a wand on front. From the outside, the book didn't look all that special. It was the adventures inside that made Gwendolyn's Magical Tales priceless, at least to me.

I smiled remembering Aunt Thelma perched on the end of my bed, reading while my eyelids grew heavy and I'd drift off to sleep. It was in those moments, snuggled under my pink duvet, surrounded by my stuffed animals and the soft glow of my bedside lamp, that I'd never felt more cozy and safe. After I'd lost my mom, I'd felt adrift, but Aunt Thelma had anchored me, reading to me every night. I could count on those stories, and little by little, I had learned I could count on my aunt, too. She'd do everything she could to make me feel loved and protected.

I was holding onto the image so tight that I didn't catch it in time.

WHACK!

The book appeared out of thin air and smacked me right in the side of the face.

"Ouch!" My hand shot up to cover my cheek. The book fell to the table with a thud.

"Are you okay?" Vance rushed forward.

Aunt Thelma sat shocked. "What in the world was that? You traced the book and conjured it at the same time! How?"

"I honestly have no idea, but I told you I loved that book." I rubbed my cheek.

"Somebody's been practicing," Aunt Thelma said over her shoulder to Vance.

"You better watch out, she'll give you a run for your money," Vance winked.

My face still stung, but I smiled at the praise. I was getting better at controlling my magic, even if it did come on a bit strong at times.

"Here," Vance held his fingertips up to my cheek. I couldn't hear the incantation, but my face quickly grew cold as if I was holding an ice pack to it.

"Better?" Vance asked after a moment.

"Much. Thanks." My eyes searched the area looking again for my phone.

Vance was one step ahead of me. He found my phone and brought it over to the table.

"I have a picture of the cipher on my phone. We can use it with the book to find out where the next clue is. Unless it leads us right to the sapphire?"

"I don't know, dear. I always assumed the stone was more protected than that."

Aunt Thelma and Vance worked to decode the message while I splashed some cold water on my face and freshened up. I had still been in my pajamas, and I wanted to be ready to roll once we knew the next clue.

Within fifteen minutes, the code was broken, and my face was officially numb. My cheek might bother me later, but right now it didn't hurt one bit.

Aunt Thelma read the message out loud. "In the darkest of days, my light will shine a beacon of hope."

I repeated the phrase, hoping it would make sense. After a moment or two, I still had nothing.

"What would be a beacon of hope around here?" Vance asked.

"It makes me think of a lighthouse, but our lake doesn't have one." Silverlake didn't need one either, unless we wanted to create a new tourist attraction. Now that was an idea.

"A beacon of hope could be someplace that holds promise, or maybe a place of refuge." Aunt Thelma spoke her thoughts out loud.

Vance tapped his pen on the kitchen table while he thought.

"What are some examples of a beacon of hope?" I asked. It wasn't a phrase you often heard.

"That's a good question. Maybe if we think of some, we'll be able to relate it to something here in Silverlake," Vance replied.

I started searching on my phone, but didn't get very far.

"The only one that I can think of is the Statue of Liberty. Standing proud on Ellis Island with her torch in the air." Aunt Thelma had a far off look in her eyes. I knew she'd visited the monument before. I hadn't seen the Statue of Liberty in person, but I could picture the image clearly. The statue was iconic.

And it turned out, that image was all I needed. "I think I know what it is. Think about it, what statue do we have around here that resembles the Statue of Liberty?"

Vance and Aunt Thelma shared a look.

I didn't wait for them to think of it. "The fountain at Wishing Well Park."

"The witch with her raised wand." Aunt Thelma jumped in.

"Exactly!" I replied. "I'd say she represents a beacon of hope, too." Silverlake was a place where a witch could be his or herself. And what did you see as you rounded the bend and drove into town? The witch statue standing in the center of the fountain. "We need to go." I stood so fast I smacked the top of my legs against the kitchen table. "Wait, what time is it? I'm supposed to work this morning."

"I'm taking care of the inn from here on out. You go solve this case and then focus on the wedding. I'm officially relieving you of your managerial duties, if only temporary," Aunt Thelma added before I could protest. "If you need reinforcements, call me and I'll ready the troops."

I leaned over and gave my aunt a kiss on the cheek. "Thank you, and it is good to see you. Sorry you had to come home to this mess."

"It's not you who needs to apologize, sweetheart." Aunt Thelma gave me a hug.

"I know. But still."

"No buts. You two get out of here and call me if you find anything."

Chapter 20

"Are you sure you don't want to call Deputy Jones?" Vance asked me on the way to the park. "You need to tell him about the break-in."

"I will, but right now we need to make sure the sapphire is safe."

Vance didn't argue, but I had a feeling he cared more about arresting the person who had attacked me versus finding Silverlake's legendary gemstone. If it was him who had been attacked, I would feel the same way.

Vance parked his truck, and we got out and walked the short distance across the verdant lawn. Morning dew and grass clippings clung to my shoes. The park was mostly empty except for a couple morning joggers and dog walkers. Come afternoon, families would crowd the park with blankets for afternoon picnics and impromptu kickball games.

Vance and I stood in front of the fountain, hands on our hips, examining the statue. It was taller than I remembered.

"Do you have a ladder?" The witch statue was easily ten feet tall. Not to mention that we had to step into the fountain in order to examine her.

"I can lift you on my shoulders?" Vance suggested.

I shrugged. That was probably our best bet. I could transform into a cat again, but climbing the statue would be a bit difficult, and if I slipped, I would end up soaking wet. Cats, even humans who were transfigured into them, really didn't like water. Not only that, but paws made it difficult to examine things. Never underestimate the importance of opposable thumbs.

Vance kicked off his shoes, rolled up his pants, and crouched down to the ground for me to climb onto his shoulders.

"Steady now," he said as he steadied my knees wrapped around his head and stood. I wobbled a little bit on his shoulders until we got our balance. It was a bit tricky as he stepped into the water and I had nothing to hold onto. I held my breath and eyed the fountain's stone perimeter. It would hurt a whole heck of a lot if we fell onto it.

"Oh, man. That's cold." Vance shivered below me.

"Not even a little bit refreshing?" I suggested.

"Not even. It's okay." Vance sloshed forward.

"Do you see anything?" he asked. My hands reached forward to steady myself against the bronze statue. I first examined her wand and then her billowing robes. My hands sliding down the smooth planes. Nothing jumped out at me. But then... "Wait, back up a little bit." Vance stepped backward before I was ready. "Whoa!" I pitched forward slightly. My hands landed on the top of Vance's head, and I gripped his hair for balance.

"Ouch." Vance winced.

"Sorry. I almost fell backward." I tried my best to adjust my balance without yanking Vance's hair or kneeing him in the side of the head. I didn't remember shoulder rides being so precarious when I was a child.

We regained our balance once again. "Okay, back it up slowly." I drew out the last word.

Vance moved at a snail's pace. My fingertips grazed the witch's hat. "That's it. Look, the hat is crooked. Just the tip."

"I can't see from here." Vance made a good point. If he tilted his chin up, he'd dump me off the back of his shoulders.

"Go forward a tiny bit. I'm trying to see if it moves."

Vance inched his way forward carefully. I had to stretch up, with my hands high above my head, to reach the top of the statue. I tried to open the hat like a lid, but it wouldn't budge. It was only when I twisted it that the tip unscrewed and came right off. I handed Vance the top. He dropped in gingerly into the fountain before securing my leg once more. "See anything?"

"No. Hang on." I felt around blindly inside the secret hiding space. My hands brushed what felt like a velvet box. At least I hoped it was a velvet box and not spiderwebs. But the box wouldn't move. Either it hadn't been designed to come out of the hat, or the box had welded itself inside with age. Regardless, it didn't freely move.

"Can you lift me a little bit higher?" I knew we were taking a risk, but I had to get my hand on the box.

"Sure. Are you ready?"

"Go for it."

Vance braced one hand against the statue and rose on his tiptoes.

I stretched as high as I could. My muscles were extended to their fullest. I wrapped my fingertips around the box and twisted, hard, like I was opening the lid on a stubborn jar of pickles. The fastener gave way and I lifted the box up.

"Got it!" I said the second my hand clasped freed the box.

Vance wasted no time getting us out of the fountain and then back to the ground. The box was a rectangle about four inches long and two inches wide with hinges on the back.

"It's probably empty," I remarked. Clearly, someone had already been here.

"Let's open it and find out."

I looked at Vance and then back down at the box and creaked it open. I was right, it was empty, but the item inside had left an indentation in the bottom of the box. The material reminded me of the green florist foam. The foam had acted to protect the clue inside, nestling it for a century and then some. I wasn't sure how long ago the founding fathers hid the sapphire. I could've been right when the town was founded, or years later.

"Look at that." I motioned to the indentation.

"It was a key."

"And there's an engraving on the inside of the lid." I had to hold the box at the right angle in order to read the script. It read, "Let no man put asunder." I said the phrase word by word as I made them out. "What is that from?" I said to Vance.

"Put asunder," Vance repeated.

"Let no man put asunder." I repeated it.

"Why is that familiar?"

"We just heard it, didn't we? Where did we hear that?" Don't you hate when you know something is familiar to you, but you can't remember from where.

Vance was one step ahead of me. He got out his

smart phone and searched the phrase online. "It's from a wedding ceremony." He turned his phone to me for me to see.

"That's right. Father George said it at the rehearsal. What God has joined, let no man put asunder."

"What does that mean here, though?"

"Maybe it's the church, given the religious connotation. Unless you can think of something that's separated around here? Isn't that what put asunder means? Let no man separate?"

"I'm not sure about anything separating, but it would be smart to check the church first. Maybe we'll get lucky and catch the thief in the act."

It only took a handful of minutes for us to drive around the lake to reach the church. I blinked at the packed parking lot. With everything that had happened, I'd forgotten today was Sunday.

"Should we wait?" Vance asked.

I thought about it for a minute. Would the thief wait? Probably not. They would most likely relish the fact that it was packed. Vance and I should do the same. "No, let's use the service as cover. It might help us blend in."

But I faltered as soon as I said those words.

I looked up at the imposing church. Suddenly, the task seemed monumental. "How are we going to find this lock?" Seeing the clue was a key, I assumed we needed to find what it opened.

"We'll just take it one room at a time. If we don't find anything by the time the service gets out, we can ask Father George what he thinks."

"Good idea." I couldn't freak out and think that it was an impossible task. If I did that, we would never find the sapphire or who was behind the string of murders and theft. That wasn't an option.

I was trying not to look and act suspicious but failed miserably with the way I held my wand out. I wasn't about to get attacked from behind, not again. We stepped inside the church and heard the organ reverberating from the second floor where the choir also sang.

The service was almost over. I could tell it was at the offertory portion based upon the music being played.

Diane's husband, Roger, was one of the ushers. He and Diane had helped out on more than one case, and I knew I could trust him.

"Is everything okay?" Roger whispered. The sanctuary was separated from the entry hall by two heavy wooden doors. We could hear Father George's voice through the wood.

"Not really. We're working a case, and a clue led us here. I'm trying to find something to unlock."

"The last clue was a key," Vance clarified.

"We didn't see it, and we don't know what it goes to. And it might not even belong to anything in the church."

"Well, that's a pretty tall order. Let me think. Father George's office has a lock as does the secretary's. There's a small safe in there for deposits." My ears perked up at the sound of that. Could the Silverlake Sapphire be in the church's safe?

"Does the safe take a key?" I asked.

"Oh no, sorry. It has a combination lock. Bonnie counts the money after the service and puts the deposit together and stores it in there until Father George takes it to the bank."

"Okay, so it's not the safe."

My cell phone started to ring, and I quickly got that panicky expression on my face. It was the look you get when your phone goes off at the most inopportune times, like in the middle of a church service, for example. I silenced my phone but then decided I better answer it when I saw that it was Aunt Thelma calling.

"Hang on, let me take this." I stepped outside onto the steps and hit answer.

"Hello?"

"If you ever want to see your aunt alive again, step away from the church right now." The voice sounded altered, like it was spoken through a computer synthesizer.

"Excuse me? Who is this? What's going on?"

"You heard me."

The ringtone on my phone changed, signaling an incoming video call. I hit accept, and my aunt's image filled the screen. She had her mouth taped shut and her wrists bound behind her back. I couldn't tell where she was at, but it looked like she was sitting on a cement floor. "Aunt Thelma!"

The video went dead, and the voice returned.

"You and your boyfriend head back to the inn. I have eyes watching you. Once I get the sapphire, I'll tell you where your aunt is. You call the police, she's dead. You come looking for me, she's dead. Do you understand?"

I nodded, unable to speak.

"Good," the voice replied, and then the line went dead.

I walked back to Vance on shaky legs. He and Roger both rushed to my side. "What's wrong?" Vance still kept his voice low.

"Nothing. Everything's fine." I couldn't even lie well at that moment. My voice sounded shaky and off pitch. "I need to talk to Vance for a moment. Excuse us."

Roger nodded and Vance and I walked back outside.

"Are you going to tell me what's wrong?" Vance said as we stood on the church's front steps.

I took a steadying breath. "Aunt Thelma's been kidnapped."

Chapter 21

Vance and I were back at the inn, waiting for the kidnapper to call back. Right then I didn't care about the sapphire or solving the case, I only cared about getting my aunt back safe and sound.

Emily had been working with Aunt Thelma when she'd stepped outside to take the trash out. That was all it took for the kidnapper to act.

I didn't tell Emily what had happened, though. Instead, I told her Aunt Thelma ran into an old friend and asked if I'd finish her shift. My aunt was a social butterfly, and seeing she'd been out of town for so long, the story was believable.

But as the minutes ticked by and there was still no word on Aunt Thelma, I grew frantic. What if the person found the sapphire and had already left town, not bothering to call? Should I do a tracking spell? I'd be able to find her, but what if the kidnapper was still in town and found out, and killed her? I felt like I had no good options and the wait was making me insane.

"Are you holding up okay?" Vance wrapped his arm around me.

"No," I confessed. "A million what ifs are playing through my head, and I'm worried I'm making the wrong choice."

"You don't want to wait." It wasn't a question.

"I don't want to screw up. I want to do whatever brings Aunt Thelma home safely. I just don't know what that is." I needed to have my wits about me. Now wasn't the time to get panicky.

I thought some more. It had been a couple hours since the phone call. What had the kidnapper said exactly? I replayed what I could remember from the conversation, looking for clues.

You and your boyfriend head back to the inn. That phrase stuck out to me.

"They could see us. They said you and I needed to leave the church."

"Do you think they were at the church?"

"Possibly. I'm thinking up high maybe." I then remembered something else. "I didn't reply to the demands. When they asked me if I understood, I was only able to nod, but they replied *good.*"

"They could really see you then."

"Think about it. Where could they be up high at the church and still see me?"

Vance didn't need to think long. "The bell tower."

"Exactly. The only problem is the kidnapper isn't working alone. We already know that from my attack and they said they had eyes watching us. Who could be working together?"

"It could be Mr. Montgomery and another one of his crew members."

"I suppose." Deputy Jones never got back with me on Mr. Montgomery's background check. "The history teacher, Mr. Skyler is pretty suspicious, too."

"He was out at The Crossroads."

"Maybe he's a shifter, hence the black cat, and one of the teenage boys is helping him?"

"Not sure why he'd break into his own class-room, though."

Neither Vance nor I had an answer for that.

Vance's cell phone rang and it caused me to jump. My hopes skyrocketed for a second until Vance said that it was Dottie down at the sheriff department.

"Don't say anything!" I hissed.

Vance shook his head. "No, I won't." He then turned his attention back to the phone. I couldn't help but eavesdrop.

"You got a name?" Vance replied. I watched as he fumbled for a piece of paper behind the desk and scribbled something down. "An archaeologist. You have to be kidding me."

"Archaeologist?"

Vance held up a finger, signaling he was almost done. "Okay, Dottie, I sure appreciate it. Thank you so much. Bye now." Vance clicked off.

"What's going on and how did you get Dottie to feed you info?"

"Dottie has a crush on our very own fire chief Brody. I introduced them, so she owed me. Our mystery guy on the Enchanted Trail, the professor? His name was Samuel Yates. He was an archeologist professor specializing in geology."

"As in gems?"

Vance nodded. "Get this, his research paper? It was on the Silverlake Sapphire."

"His death wasn't an accident." Deputy Jones was wrong and I shouldn't have dropped it.

"Nope. They got the medical report back, too. Dottie says he was cursed."

My mind raced to catch up and put the pieces together. "We need to find out more about this Samuel guy. See if he's connected to Mr. Montgomery or Mr. Skyler. He's linked to whoever the killer is. We know it wasn't random."

"I'll see what I can find." Vance retrieved my laptop from the back office and hopped online to begin his search.

I watched his fingers fly across the keyboard, but I still felt like he wasn't moving fast enough. It wasn't his fault, I was just tired of sitting around waiting for answers. Whoever had my aunt most likely had killed Mr. Craddock, Derek, and Samuel. I couldn't cross my fingers and hope they'd do the right thing now and release Aunt Thelma once they had the sapphire. Why would they? Especially if she'd seen their face.

"You keep looking. We'll need a paper trail. I'm going to the church. Not as myself," I added before Vance could interrupt. "I'm heading out as a cat. You stay here, because I'm sure they're watching the inn."

"Wait—"

"Don't worry, I'll be safe. I'm only going to ID the kidnappers and then come back." Cats might have nine lives, but I wasn't sure how many I'd already used, and I didn't plan to lose another one today.

I TRANSFORMED into a cat and snuck out the door when a guest opened it. If anyone had been watching, I'd look like an ordinary cat sneaking about, because let's be honest, cats are curious by nature.

The easiest way for me to get to the church was by taking the Enchanted Trail. It would take me a bit longer in feline form, but I was determined to get there as quickly as possible.

What I hadn't been counting on was the black cat giving chase. I was halfway around the lake, making good time at a steady pace. I wasn't running because I hadn't wanted to draw attention to myself, but that was all about to change.

I looked behind my shoulder in the nick of time. The black cat jumped out in an ambush. It came flying out of the bushes, claws outstretched, ready to dig into me. I veered to the right, my paws dug into the wood chips and sent them spraying behind me. The black cat missed me by mere inches.

I gave a yowl and then took off like a bolt of lightning.

The black cat didn't back down. I couldn't have run any faster if the devil himself was nipping at my tail. I sprinted as fast as my four legs could carry me. I hadn't planned on running the entire Enchanted Trail, but psycho cat didn't give me much of a choice.

I veered off the path, trying to lose the other cat, but it never gave up. I was trying to decide what to do. Maybe I could run up to the first person I saw for help. If I stayed as a cat, the psycho cat wouldn't be able to do much if someone picked me up and I could still remain undercover.

But I didn't see anyone in sight as the church came into view. I panicked, unsure of what to do. If only I'd come sooner when the congregation was still milling about.

I was running up the church steps, staring at the windowsill as a possible escape, when a hand grabbed my foot. The black cat behind me had morphed back into their human form and Jeff Harcourt gripped my ankle, hard.

Without even thinking, I too changed back. Everything happened in a blur, but I knew it would be harder for him to run off with me if I was in human form. I scrambled back and used my free leg to kick the man in the face. Then, in one fluid motion, I withdrew my wand and yelled, "Artiko Maximus!" It was a super strength freezing charm. I must've really wanted to stop the man, because he turned into a solid block of ice, right there on the church's steps.

I was feeling pretty proud of myself until I heard the revolver cock back.

"Move and I shoot," Cecilia said from the cracked doorway.

"C'mon, Cecilia. It's over, everyone can see your husband is a popsicle out here. It'll only be minutes until the sheriff finds out, too."

"Then you better make it quick." Cecilia opened the door further and revealed Aunt Thelma bound on the floor. "Unless you want me to shoot her?" Cecilia turned the gun on my aunt.

My heart leapt into my throat. I felt pretty good about my chances to out run Cecilia, but not when she had my aunt hostage. "Stop! I'm coming."

Cecilia lowered the gun and held open the church's oversized wooden door for me to enter. She locked the door after us.

"Up now," she said, nudging Aunt Thelma with her shoe.

My aunt scowled. I couldn't imagine what she was thinking. She didn't even know Cecilia and Jeffery, and here they'd kidnapped her? I could imagine how it had played out. Cecilia asked Aunt Thelma directions to the park, and the next thing you know, Jeffery's stunned her or some such. Aunt Thelma is so friendly and trusting, she never would've seen it coming.

"What spell did you hit Jeffery with?" Cecilia said as she walked behind us, forcing us up the narrow stairwell.

I shrugged my shoulders. I wasn't about to help this woman out at all.

"No matter. Let him melt. I don't need him anymore anyway."

I was shocked at how easily Cecelia dismissed her husband. She was the coldblooded one. I had no doubt.

"Turns out keeping you alive came in handy. If you were dead, I couldn't force you to do this."

"D-do what?" I hated how my voice shook. We were at the top of the bell tower, or so I thought. A rickety wooden ladder had been propped up against the wall. I could see a key dangling from the ceiling.

It looked like a trapdoor. The kind you would install to access an attic.

"I couldn't get it to open, but now I think I know why. A descendent of the founding fathers has to unlock it, doesn't it?" Cecelia looked down at Aunt Thelma. She glared. "I'm right, aren't I? It's just the type of ridiculous magic this little Podunk town would come up with. Now up!" Cecelia pointed the gun at my chest.

"I'm going. You can drop the gun."

"Not on your life," and then she laughed at her twisted sense of humor before turning serious. "I said move it." She motioned with the gun up the stairs.

I took my time climbing the ladder, wondering where on earth they'd stored this thing. The wood was splintered and creaked with every step. I prayed it wouldn't giveaway and send me crashing to the stone floor below.

Eventually I made it to the top where the trap-door was. I made sure to keep my eyes forward. Heights and I didn't mix when I was a human. I'd rather be a cat climbing this ladder any day.

The lock easily released as if someone opened it everyday, and I was able to slide the wood up and over. The space was only big enough for me to stick my head or my hand through, but not both.

I glanced up into it. The space was dusty and dark, but there it was. A sapphire, glowing brilliant blue, reflecting off late afternoon sun. It sat on a gold metal stand, positioned so the sun and moon beams could shine on it. I had to lower my head and reach through with my arm. My fingers reached out, and I felt around blindly knowing the general direction of the gem. As soon as my fingertips touched it, they began to tingle with the immense power. It was almost too much to hold on to. Instinct told me to let go, but I plucked the gem from the stand anyway. I could only hope the power would overcome Cecelia and I'd be able to take her out when she wasn't expecting it.

I descended the stairs. I felt like I was floating the entire time. My hand vibrated and my ears rang.

"Give me the stone," Cecelia practically growled, snatching the stone from my hand before I'd even stepped off the ladder. The aggressive move caused me to miss the last two rungs and land sideways on my ankle.

I winced. Nerves shot up my leg. I hobbled, trying to walk it off and get to my aunt as quickly as possible.

I looked over at Cecelia. A moment of triumph filled the mad woman's eyes. "I got it. I did it!" She looked at me, proud of herself. The woman was delusional in addition to being a coldhearted killer.

I wanted to reach for my wand and take her out. Now was the perfect opportunity.

But something better happened. A moment after the evil woman had the stone in her possession, a loud roar ripped through the sky. Followed by another. Something swooped outside the bell tower as if it was circling us in the air like a predator.

"What is that?" Cecelia stammered, looking frightened as shadows outside the window grew more menacing.

She took her gun and pointed it out the archway, aiming for the unseen attacker.

It was my turn to smile wickedly. I knew exactly what they were, and our town's founders were brilliant.

Rocky swooped into the opened archway and tackled Cecelia. Hitting her right in the chest with his massive paws. She held firmly to the sapphire, but she was no match to the gargoyle's strength. Cecelia screamed as the weight of the beast landed on her chest. I had been in her position before. Rocky had pinned my down and stood before me, his eyes glowing red. Drool slipping out of his jowls, and pooling against my neck. It was terrifying stuff. I shouldn't be enjoying Cecelia's distress, but it felt like poetic justice.

It wasn't until the second gargoyle, the one fire chief Brody had named Zeus, joined in and yanked the sapphire out of Cecelia's hand with his mouth. It was then that I knew the gemstone would well and truly be safe. Cecelia had no idea that the gargoyles were friendly, or they would be if you weren't attempting to steal from the town.

"Good boy, Rocky." I went over and patted the friendly beast on his head. This paws still held Cecelia in place. I looked down at Cecelia, and she was passed out cold.

Chapter 22

Cecelia and her husband, Jeffrey, were charged with the murder of Samuel Yates, Thomas Craddock and Derek Sawyer. They were also charged with five counts of breaking and entering and one count of grand theft involving the jewelry store. Jefferey had sung like a canary. He was against the whole treasure hunting business from the onset, but he loved his wife to a fault. To Cecelia, the Silverlake Sapphire was another adventure. Once she set her sights on it, she would stop at nothing until she obtained it.

The Harcourts heard about the legend from Samuel, but they didn't know the details other than the location. Cecelia killed Samuel when showed up in Silverlake to hunt for the sapphire himself. She couldn't have him blow their cover. But without Samuel's information, the Harcourts were forced to look for the history book. Even after they got their hands on the cipher, they didn't know who had the book or who the founding families of Silverlake were. The history book led them right to my apartment courtesy of a photo of our great, great, great Aunt Ida Nightingale.

The only thing Mr. Skyler was guilty of was growing up in The Crossroads. He was embarrassed about where he came from, and was determined to make the community a better place than it was when he'd lived there, hence the tutoring sessions.

As for Gabby and her brother, he was bitter his grandfather hadn't left them much money. He was always under the impression that he'd inherit his grandfather's considerable wealth, but the older man left the majority of it to area charities. It didn't bother Gabby, but her brother couldn't let it go. Rumor had it, he was still fighting the will in probate court.

The only mystery that remained unsolved was who turned Harvey into stone.

The Harcourts admitted to hiring Harvey to steal the cipher, and they had set him up to take the fall for the jewelry store as well, but they were adamant they didn't turn him into stone. It wasn't until much later, when the curse hadn't yet worn off, that Loretta confessed to cursing her grandson.

"I knew he was in trouble. That this time he was in way over his head. I cursed him to keep him safe," she confessed to me while I was working the front desk at the inn. "Now I don't know what to do!"

I too was at a loss for words, but it was fortunate that I knew a lot of smart witches who could solve some really tough cases.

"Have you talked to Connie?"

"The potion master?"

"You never know, Connie is brilliant. Maybe she can help you." Loretta looked skeptical. "Would it help if I came with you?" I wanted to talk with Connie about a wedding gift. I hadn't forgotten my plan, I just hadn't had time to ask about it yet.

"Maybe a little."

"Go on," Aunt Thelma said, coming out of the back office. She was true to her word, and I was officially not working until after the wedding. Let's be realistic here, I didn't know what to do with myself if I wasn't working. Thankfully, Aunt Thelma didn't give me too much grief when I checked in a guest or two or took care of some paperwork in the office.

Loretta and I left the inn and went straight to Mix it Up! to see what we could find.

Chapter 23

One week later...

It was just before Percy and Eleanor went to cut the cake that I pulled them aside.

"Before you do that, there's something that I want you to try." I held out a square box for Percy to open.

Percy looked at me questioningly. I really hoped this would work. Percy held the box while Eleanor lifted the lid. Together they peered inside at the lavender perfume bottle. The color was irrelevant to the spell. I had chosen it to match the couple's wedding colors.

"Now, the effects aren't permanent, but it should bring a little bit more joy to your life." I said cryptically.

"What is it?" Eleanor asked.

"A surprise. Now here, open your mouth and

say, ahhhhhh." Percy was too curious to resist. As soon as he stuck out his tongue, I sprayed two pumps full of the liquid into his mouth. I turned to Eleanor. "Do you want to try?"

"I suppose so." Elinor copied Percy, and I sprayed her mouth as well.

"Now, go taste your cake," I instructed.

"Will I be—?" Percy was too excited to finish his sentence.

"Only one way to find out," I smiled, broadly.

Guests all gathered around the table as Percy and Eleanor placed hand over hand on the cutting knife and sunk it into the cake.

"If this works, Jelly, I promise to never prank you again," Percy said with heavy emotion. I'd never heard the poltergeist sound so serious in my whole entire life.

"Now, don't go being ridiculous," I started to say, but the poltergeist hadn't heard me.

"Oh my. This is good," he moaned. "It's even better than I remembered. This is officially the greatest day in my life." I looked at Eleanor to see how she would react to Percy's claim, but she was too busy closing her eyes and savoring the sweet buttercream.

"What is that spray?" Eleanor asked when she opened her eyes.

"It's a tasting spray. Connie mixed it up for me." Along with a potion for Loretta. All she had to do was pour it over Harvey's head and leave him out under the full moon, and voilà, Harvey was back to his normal self, although his skin was still a bit dry. Nothing a good moisturizer couldn't cure. Loretta had been so concerned with her grandson's safety that she had blasted him with one heck of a gargoyle charm. It was another reminder of how much magic and emotions were tied together.

Loretta was wrong about a couple things, though. Harvey wasn't completely innocent. Not only did he steal the book cipher, but also the pearl ring. And he stole the ring all on his own, hoping to make a quick buck. I hoped Harvey had learned his lesson after getting involved with the Harcourts, but who knew.

"You did it," Vance slipped beside me and took my hand in his. "Walk with me?" I allowed Vance to tug me out of the reception and into the afternoon air. "Was the wedding a success?"

"I'd say so."

"You did good."

"Thank you."

Vance and I walked and talked about the week, how crazy it was, the emotional roller coasters, and how we were thankful to have each other. We needed the time to ourselves. It felt good to reconnect and be together without tracking down clues and eliminating suspects.

Before I knew it, we were standing in front of the fountain once more.

"We've had a lot of moments at this fountain." Vance was right, we had. We'd played in the water as children, snuck kisses behind it as teenagers, and even broke up standing before it. So many memories. Some good, some not so good, but all of them woven together to tell our story.

"I've been thinking about that clue. The one that said the statue was a beacon of hope." Vance took both of my hands in his own and turned to face me. "You, Angelica, are my beacon of hope. In the midst of darkness, you are a shining light. When I look at us together, I see so many promises. I want to reach out, grab them, and never let go. There is no one else I want beside me from here until eternity."

"What are you saying?" My heart fluttered in my chest like the butterflies dancing in my tummy, but I didn't want to get ahead of myself. I wanted to make sure Vance was saying what I thought he was.

"I'm saying that I don't want to only wake up next to you tomorrow, but I want all of your tomorrows." Vance tipped up my chin. "Look at me. You are maddening, but in the best way possible. I don't want to change you. I love how your mind works. You have beauty, brains, and the biggest heart. I'd be lost without you. I love you."

"I love you too." I smiled.

Vance squeezed my hands. "Angelica? Will you marry me?"

This wasn't the first time Vance had proposed. The last time had been fourteen years ago. We'd been kids back then. I can't even remember what he had said.We had grown so much since that time that I could irrevocably say that Vance was the man for me. "There's nothing in this world I would love more. Yes, I'll marry you."

Vance leaned in and sealed the promise with a kiss.

Now, if only trouble could permanently vacate Silverlake the world would truly be a beautiful place. Was that too much to ask for?

Probably.

But with Vance at my side, we'd tackle whatever came next.

READY FOR THE next Mystic Inn? Check out Book 7 in the series: **https://books2read.com/u/bxJ8Rv**

Stephanie Damore Complete Works

Mystic Inn Mysteries
Witchy Reservations (FREE)
Eerie Check In
Spooked Solid
Untimely Departure
Midnight at Mystic Inn
Bewitched Break Inn
Potions, Poison, and Pumpkin Spice

SPIRITED SWEETS MYSTERIES
Bittersweet Betrayal (FREE)
Decadent Demise

Red Velvet Revenge
Sugared Suspect
Indulgent Injury

WITCH IN TIME

Better Witch Next Time (FREE)
Play for Time
Time Will Tell

BEAUTY SECRETS SERIES

Makeup & Murder (FREE)
Kiss & Makeup
Eyeliner & Alibis
Pedicures & Prejudice
Beauty & Bloodshed
Charm & Deception

About the Author

Stephanie Damore is a USA Today bestselling mystery author with a soft spot for magic and romance, too. She loves being on the beach, has a strong affinity for the color pink (especially in diamonds and champagne), and, not to brag, but chocolate and her are in a pretty serious relationship.

Her books are fun and fearless, and feature smart and sassy sleuths. If you love books with a dash of romance and twist of whodunit, you're going to love her work!

For information on new releases and fun giveaways, visit her Facebook group: Paranormal Mystery Coven

https://www.facebook.com/groups/213139283675694

facebook.com/stephdamoreauthor

twitter.com/stephdamore

instagram.com/steph_damore_author

bookbub.com/profile/stephanie-damore